W9-BNX-172

He hesitated. "Are we going to talk about it?"

Her cheeks pinkened. "You mean—"

"The kiss that left me aching for you."

That light flush became even darker. She was so cute when she blushed.

"If that alarm call hadn't come through, what do you think would have happened next?" Davis asked, curious. He knew what he'd *wanted* to happen but...

"I would have told you good-night. The same way I'm doing now."

His lips quirked. He turned away from her. *Shot down.*

"Davis, you don't want the trouble I bring."

Her low words had him glancing back at her. "I can handle trouble. It's kind of my specialty."

Jamie took a step back. "But..."

"Let's be clear. I want you like damn hell on fire right now. I've been fantasizing about you for months. When I finally got my hands on you tonight...well, the desire I felt just got stronger. I want you."

RECKONINGS

New York Times Bestselling Author
CYNTHIA EDEN

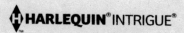
HARLEQUIN® INTRIGUE®

If you purchased this book without a cover you should be aware that this book is stolen property. It was reported as "unsold and destroyed" to the publisher, and neither the author nor the publisher has received any payment for this "stripped book."

For my wonderful friend Joan…
thanks so much for all of your encouragement! You are the best!

ISBN-13: 978-0-373-74914-0

Reckonings

Copyright © 2015 by Cindy Roussos

Recycling programs
for this product may
not exist in your area.

All rights reserved. Except for use in any review, the reproduction or utilization of this work in whole or in part in any form by any electronic, mechanical or other means, now known or hereinafter invented, including xerography, photocopying and recording, or in any information storage or retrieval system, is forbidden without the written permission of the publisher, Harlequin Enterprises Limited, 225 Duncan Mill Road, Don Mills, Ontario M3B 3K9, Canada.

This is a work of fiction. Names, characters, places and incidents are either the product of the author's imagination or are used fictitiously, and any resemblance to actual persons, living or dead, business establishments, events or locales is entirely coincidental.

This edition published by arrangement with Harlequin Books S.A.

For questions and comments about the quality of this book, please contact us at CustomerService@Harlequin.com.

® and TM are trademarks of Harlequin Enterprises Limited or its corporate affiliates. Trademarks indicated with ® are registered in the United States Patent and Trademark Office, the Canadian Intellectual Property Office and in other countries.

Printed in U.S.A.

www.Harlequin.com

Cynthia Eden, a *New York Times* bestselling author, writes tales of romantic suspense and paranormal romance. Her books have received starred reviews from *Publishers Weekly*, and she has received a RITA® Award nomination for best romantic suspense novel. Cynthia lives in the Deep South, loves horror movies and has an addiction to chocolate. More information about Cynthia may be found at cynthiaeden.com, or you can follow her on Twitter, @cynthiaeden.

Visit the Author Profile page at
Harlequin.com for more titles.

CAST OF CHARACTERS

Jamie Myers—Dr. Jamie Myers has spent years running from her past. She left her family and tried to start a new life, but she still hasn't managed to escape from her nightmares. A dangerous stalker has found Jamie, and he isn't going to stop, not until she's his...or she's dead.

Davis McGuire—Fierce ex-SEAL Davis McGuire can tell that Jamie is afraid, and when she comes to McGuire Securities looking for a bodyguard, he immediately takes the job. He is more than ready for any threat that comes his way. Davis isn't the hands-off type, and he's determined to protect Jamie both day...and night.

Sullivan McGuire—The youngest brother in the McGuire family, Sullivan is the one who feels the most protective toward his family. He doesn't trust Jamie, not completely, and he intends to make certain that she can't hurt his brother. Sullivan suspects that Jamie is keeping secrets from Davis—maybe outright lying to the other man—and he sets out to uncover the *real* truth about her mysterious past.

Henry Westport—Wealthy Henry nearly destroyed Jamie's life once before. According to Henry's family and his doctors, Henry is no longer a threat, not to anyone. But Jamie still cannot think of Henry without terror flooding through her, and she isn't so sure that he has changed... Can a killer ever truly change?

Sylvia Jones—Sylvia has been working as Jamie's assistant for a long time—long enough to know that Jamie has been hiding deep secrets. But when danger begins to stalk Jamie, Sylvia's life is also threatened. Being close to Jamie can be a very hazardous situation.

Sean Nyle—Jamie's ex-lover hasn't let the past go. He betrayed Jamie once, and he may be setting up the scene to betray her again. He claims that he wants to atone for his past mistakes, but Jamie knows just how deceptive he can truly be. Sean always has an angle, and when he appears in her life again, trouble immediately follows him.

Chapter One

Everyone loved a good wedding. Or at least, people were supposed to love a wedding. And the wedding that she'd just watched had certainly been incredible. The bride, Ava McGuire, had been glowing as she took the hand of her husband, Mark Montgomery. The guests had erupted into cheers when the couple was pronounced man and wife. Shouts and whistles had filled the air when the two kissed.

Yes, everyone was supposed to love a wedding.

But Jamie Myers had spent the past hour wishing she could slip away from the crowd. Wishing she could pretty much be anywhere else. Sure, she liked both Ava and Mark. They were great people. It was just…the crowd. All the noise. The voices. The people.

And seeing what I'll never have.

The big family. The ease, the comfort that

came from that connection. It was too much. Because Jamie stared at all of them, and she remembered what she'd lost.

"Time to throw the bouquet!"

Jamie flinched. Scarlett McGuire had shouted the announcement as she strode past Jamie, and now she was flashing a rather wicked grin her way, as if she realized Jamie would rather walk through hell than make a grab for that bouquet. Of all the women at that wedding reception, Scarlett probably knew Jamie the best. *So she knows this is when I'll run.*

Jamie tried to inch away, but a swarm of other women and a cloud of perfume surrounded her. She was pushed forward. Pushed up closer to the bride.

No, no, no! She threw up her hands, trying to knock the bouquet away when it actually came right at her.

Jamie thought she heard a sharp bark of male laughter, and she realized that she'd squeezed her eyes shut. Jamie cracked open one eye just in time to see the bouquet bounce off her hand and fly toward one of the bridesmaids. The woman let out a shriek of joy and fist-pumped like a football player who'd just crossed into the end zone.

Jamie felt a surge of relief. The crowd

thinned. It was finally late enough for her to leave the party and head back to the safety of her little house and—

"I've never seen anyone actually hit a bouquet *away* quite like that," a deep, dark male voice drawled. "Got to say, it was impressive. I bet you would make one hell of a volleyball player."

Her gaze slid to the left, and she found trouble. Right there. The tall, broad-shouldered man with the thick, dark hair and the glinting green eyes... Oh, yes, he was definitely trouble.

He was also one of the bride's brothers.

Davis McGuire lifted one brow as he stared at her. His hair was a bit darker than Ava's, and while Ava was a beautiful woman... Davis was one dangerous-looking man. His face was hard angles—high cheekbones, a square jaw. In the time that she'd been in Texas, Jamie wasn't sure she'd ever seen the guy smile. He just oozed a brooding intensity. An intensity that frightened her.

Because I've seen trouble like him before. And she still had the scars from that encounter.

But when she gazed at Davis, Jamie didn't feel afraid. She felt oddly...good. Right. *He's here now.* Such a strange thought to have. One that didn't really make sense to her.

The bride and groom rushed away in a hail of laughter and well wishes. Jamie waved to them, caught for a moment by the joy that she could see on Ava's face. Ava had certainly lived through her own hell—she deserved every bit of the happiness that she had.

Don't we all deserve to be happy?

And then…the bride and groom were gone. Riding off to their happy-ever-after ending.

Some people actually got those.

Others didn't. Others got nightmares. Jamie shivered.

Davis stepped closer to her. "I'm guessing it's safe to say that you're not real interested in getting married right now."

"I… It's very safe to say that." Her words trembled. She hated that sign of weakness. She straightened her shoulders and stretched her spine. Even in the heels, she only stood at about five feet six inches tall, so she was nowhere close to Davis's towering height. *At least six foot three. Maybe more.*

His head cocked as he studied her. "You look…very, very nice tonight, Doc." Male appreciation lit his gaze as it swept over her blue dress, a blue that she knew matched her eyes. "But I've got to say—" his gaze rose back to her face "—I'll never forget the way you handled that bouquet." And he smiled.

An actual, serious smile.

In that instant, his face went from dangerous to drop-dead gorgeous. She even thought that she saw a dimple wink in his cheek.

Davis offered his arm to her. "Want to dance?"

She'd met Davis shortly after moving to the area. His family owned the McGuire ranch, but the ranch itself only had a few horses on it. Jamie was a veterinarian, and she'd been called out a couple of times to check on those animals. She'd spoken briefly with Davis on each visit.

Davis didn't have a passion for the ranch. Like his brothers, he spent most of his time working at McGuire Securities, a private investigation firm in Austin. She knew he was ex-military and she'd also heard rumors about him being an adrenaline junkie who thrived on the thrill of a dangerous hunt—

"Jamie?" Davis murmured. "It wasn't a hard question. Do you want to dance?"

Her gaze cut to the crowded dance floor. "There's...so many people out there." She shook her head and eased back a step. "I don't... Um, it's probably not a good idea. Not in that crush."

Before she could turn and flee—and Jamie was giving a full-out run serious consideration—Davis caught her hand in his. At his touch, she stilled because she was pretty sure she felt a surge of heat snake from her fingers straight to her heart. Her breath caught, and her gaze shot up to meet his.

He still had that faint smile on his face. "I don't like the crowds, either. But I do know a good dance spot. Come with me, and I'll show you."

She shouldn't. Really.

But she found herself walking with him. She hadn't taken a starlit stroll with a man in...

Jamie's shoulders tensed, and she immediately shut down that thought. "I should go. I have calls in the morning and—"

"Are you afraid of me?" He'd already led her away from the crowd. They were out at the McGuire ranch because Ava had wanted her wedding to be there. She'd wanted to turn a place of tragedy into a place of joy again.

"Of course not." Jamie was very good at lying. Too good, most days. But when your life was a lie, you had to learn how to adapt quickly.

"Good." He kept walking, and he also kept his hold on her hand. A few moments later, they'd left the party behind and were beneath the tall branches of a tree that overlooked the lake on the ranch. The decorators had really gone above and beyond out there—they'd put up twinkling lights everywhere, and they looked like little stars nestled in the tree. The music drifted in the air, easily reaching them, as Davis turned and pulled her into his arms. "How about we dance right here?"

"I, um, don't think my heels were made to dance out there. It's—"

He bent. His hand slid her shoe right off. Then his fingers were gently lifting her other ankle. Lightly rubbing the flesh. Making her breath catch. And just like that, her other high heel was gone, too.

"Better?"

Her brows rose. "If dancing barefoot is better, then, yes." It was a good thing the night wasn't cold.

He laughed, the sound a little rusty but oddly warming. He put her shoes down and wrapped his hands around her waist.

"Don't expect fancy moves," she told him. Once upon a time, she'd danced in ballrooms. She'd learned all the right steps to take. But that had been years ago, and she'd stayed as far from ballrooms as possible since then.

"I don't expect anything but for you to just let go. Relax with me a bit."

Right. Because she was supposed to relax while Davis McGuire held her tightly. His body was so hard, muscled, against hers. His right hand held hers, cradling it lightly, and she could feel the edge of calluses on his fingers. Davis was a man used to hard work.

Hard work and danger.

"You smell so sweet." His voice was even deeper. Rumbling. She could almost feel that voice inside her.

"It's, um, lavender. My body lotion." And that was so not a savvy, sophisticated thing to say back to him. But her sophisticated days were long gone. Not that she'd really had them, anyway. But every part of the life she'd led was gone.

He pulled her even closer. "I like your hair down. Usually, you keep it in that little twist at your nape. I didn't even realize how long it was."

And she hadn't even realized he'd noticed her hair. Davis hadn't seemed to pay her that much attention when she visited the ranch to tend to his animals. Sure, he'd been there each time she'd come out, and that was a little surprising since she knew he worked so much in Austin, but—

"You're a million miles away," Davis said.

Jamie shook her head. "No, I'm right here." She'd put her head on his chest. It had seemed so natural to do that. The music was soft, romantic, and their bodies were swaying together. She wasn't nervous. Wasn't scared. She was just…

Almost happy.

"If I said I wanted to kiss you…" Davis murmured, "would you tell me to go to hell or…?"

She tensed. "Do you want to kiss me?"

"You're a beautiful woman, Doc. Don't sound so surprised. I know there are plenty of men who have wanted to kiss you."

She stopped the swaying of her body and eased back, but didn't lose her hold on him. She liked touching him. Odd, when she made a point not to get physically close to too many people. "I'm not talking about plenty of men right now. I'm talking about you."

His eyes gleamed. "You're a direct woman. I like that. I don't have time for lies and tricks."

Too bad. I'm all about lies. "You're a man with secrets," she threw right back. "So don't give me that line. Everyone is more than they appear to be. We all wear masks for the world to see."

His hold tightened on her waist. "You keep surprising me. Not many people can do that."

The heat from his body was wrapping around her. Tempting her to get closer to him again. To put her head back on him, to let go, just for a little while.

"I do want to kiss you," Davis said. He seemed to be staring at her mouth, and, nervously, she wet her lips. "I've wanted that for a very long time. Probably since the first day I met you."

Was he serious? Or just trying to charm her into bed?

"But what do *you* want, Jamie?"

Ah, now he'd just called her Jamie and not "Doc" like he often did. She'd rather grown used to hearing his drawl when he used that little nickname.

And what do I want? She stared up at him and knew that—for an instant—she'd like to let go of her fear. To just feel. To just get lost in a man's arms and in his kiss. It would be wonderful to act like any other woman. To simply let go...

Do it.

Davis McGuire was one of the good guys. He and his brothers helped people. They were all ex-military. Davis was a former SEAL. Tough, but good. True hero material. Sure, the things he'd done might scare her because she realized the guy knew how to fight hard and dirty but...

He won't hurt me.

If there was any man she could trust, it should be him.

But you trusted the wrong man before.

His head lowered toward hers. "One kiss."

One. One sounded fair. Or maybe that was just the champagne talking. She found herself leaning up on her tiptoes. Clutching his shoulders. Their lips were almost touching.

Maybe it was a mistake. Maybe she'd already let things go too far. But...

One kiss. What could it hurt?

Jamie opened her mouth. Her lips pressed to his.

One kiss.

It should have been gentle. It should have been light. It shouldn't have wrecked her world. Passion like that wasn't real. It was in movies. It was—

Consuming.

His arms wrapped around her as he brought her even closer. His tongue thrust past her lips, and he kissed her deep. Kissed her hard. Kissed her as if he'd been desperate to taste her for so long.

And she kissed him the same way. As if a

flood of need had just erupted within her—
and it had. Passion burned, and she couldn't
get close enough to him. Couldn't touch him
enough. She knew desire, she'd certainly felt
it before. This was different. This was...

Jamie kept kissing him. She stopped thinking and she just felt.

THE HUNT WAS OVER.

It had been such a very long hunt. So many
miles. So many years. She'd run from him.
Hurt him. Lied to him.

But he'd found her. He'd found his Jamie
again. And it was finally time to claim her
once more.

He stared at her little house. So very far
removed from the home where she'd lived
when she was his. The stars glittered behind
the house. There were no nearby neighbors.
No one to watch out for Jamie.

No one to hear her scream.

He smiled. Would she be scared when she
saw him again? Or happy? Probably both.
After all, Jamie had been bad, so he'd have
to punish her. At first.

But he loved her. She loved him. That was
what mattered most.

He headed toward her door. This was the

first time he'd gone so close to the house. *Because it's time to have my Jamie again.*

His gaze flickered down, and he saw the welcome mat. So warm with the spray of flowers across the top. So Jamie. His head tilted back and he gazed at the wind chime that hung near her front door. His fingers lifted and brushed against that chime, sending a light peel of music drifting in the air. Then he reached for the door. Locked, of course, because Jamie was the careful sort. Quickly, he glanced under the welcome mat, hoping she'd left a key out for him.

Not there.

Like that was supposed to stop him.

He walked around her house. Found a nice, easy-to-reach window. He grabbed a rock and threw it right through that glass. The window shattered—

And an alarm split the air.

What the hell?

A dog started barking, snarling from inside the house, and he saw a very sharp pair of teeth lunge toward the broken glass, as if the beast were trying to get out of that window and come after him.

He hated dogs. Jamie knew that.

Damn her.

Backing away now because he knew the

alarm would mean the arrival of cops, he kept his eyes on that growling animal. The alarm and the dog…they wouldn't stop him. Nothing would stop him, not now. His plans had been put in careful motion. He'd be back. He'd get his Jamie again.

He'd searched long and hard for her, and she would not get away from him again.

He'd see her dead first.

DAVIS PUSHED JAMIE against the trunk of the nearby tree. The lights gleamed down on them, as her body responded—hell, the woman was about to drive him right out of his head.

He couldn't stop kissing her. Her sweet taste was making him frantic. Champagne and candy…that was what she tasted like. And she was definitely making him feel a little drunk.

He'd wanted her since the first moment he saw her. That sun-streaked blond hair, her gleaming blue eyes…and her full, sensual lips. It was her lips that had really caught his attention. Jamie had an incredible mouth. Bow-shaped, sensual—he'd wanted her mouth under his.

And now I have her.

Only he hadn't quite realized he'd go full-on nuclear once he actually got to taste her. Normally, control wasn't an issue for him, but...

He kissed her harder. Her curves pressed against him, and Jamie had plenty of perfect curves. Full breasts, round hips. She was—

Ringing.

Davis stilled. Then his head slowly lifted, mostly because Jamie was pushing against his chest. She fumbled to pull a phone from a hidden pocket in her dress—*very* hidden. Her fingers were trembling a bit; he could see that small shake clearly.

Jamie had been just as affected by that kiss as he had been. Good to know.

"I—I'm sorry," Jamie said. "But I have to take this call. It could be an emergency."

He knew she handled plenty of emergency cases in her practice. Just a few months back, she'd been called out when the groom—Mark Montgomery—had discovered that his prize stallion had been poisoned. Only Jamie's immediate response had saved that animal. Others in the area relied on her, too. Jamie was the best vet they'd seen in those parts in a very long time.

So he backed away. He sucked in a deep breath. And he adjusted his pants because he was seriously turned on by her.

Jamie put the phone to her ear. "This is Jamie Myers—" She broke off, her breath stuttering out a bit. "No, no, I'm not home." She surged away from the tree. "Yes, please, send the cops over. I'm on my way now."

He tensed. "Jamie?" Davis didn't like the sharp edge of fear that he'd heard in her voice.

She shoved her phone back into that hidden pocket and hurriedly scooped up her shoes. She didn't even pause to put them on before rushing toward the line of parked cars up on the crest.

"Jamie, wait!" He ran after her. Caught her arm and spun her around to face him. "What's happening?"

"The alarm went off at my place. It could be a break-in." She pushed his hand away. "I have to go. I'm sorry, I—"

Davis swore. "Don't be sorry. But let me come with you." A break-in...and she thought he was just going to stand back while she raced home? That wasn't his style, not at all.

"No, no, you don't have to—"

He caught her hand in his. "I want to. You take your car, and I'll follow behind you, okay? But when we get to your house, don't even think of going inside without me." Because he'd witnessed too many bad scenes before. "I need to make sure you're safe."

"Why?"

He just stared at her.

"Why does it matter to you that I'm safe?" She seemed legitimately confused about that point.

"Because you matter."

She laughed. "No, I don't." Jamie pulled away from him. "The kiss was great, amazing really."

Yes, it had been.

"But I have to go. Good night, Davis." She was running away from him. Literally.

He shook his head. She really thought he was going to let her walk—run—into danger?

Not this time.

He started jogging after her. And his brother stepped into his path.

"Whoa, whoa, slow down man," Brodie said. Brodie was Davis's twin...and folks often mistakenly thought Brodie was the more easygoing of the two. Those people were wrong. Davis knew that neither of them had the word "easy" in their vocabulary. "Where's the fire?" Brodie wanted to know.

Davis elbowed him out of the way. "At the doc's place." He pointed after Jamie. The woman had moved fast. She was already at her car. "She just got a call from her alarm company. Something set off the system. I'm going over with her."

"You need me?" Brodie shouted after him.

Because that was the way it was with his twin. Brodie had his back, always.

"Not this time," Davis called. "I'll check in when I know she's clear." He gave a quick wave over his shoulder. "It was one hell of a wedding!" *And I still can't believe our baby sister is married.* Sweet Ava...she'd finally found happiness. He'd worried about her for so many years. The pain in her eyes had torn at him. But that pain was gone now. Ava was happy. The demons of her past had been put to rest.

He knew Mark Montgomery would do everything possible to make sure that Ava never had another moment of fear or pain in her life. Mark loved Ava. She was his number one priority. A good thing...because if she hadn't been, then Davis would've needed to knock some sense into the guy—friend or no friend.

Davis reached his truck. He jumped inside and caught the flash of Jamie's taillights. The woman was driving hell-fast. She needed to slow down. "Be safe, sweetheart," he muttered as he cranked up his ride. Jamie didn't realize how serious the situation could be.

He knew that danger waited, though. Even

in the so-called safe places, like in the home where you let down your guard, danger could be hidden.

Once upon a time, he'd thought his ranch was the safest place on earth. He'd left the ranch, gone all over the world to fight and taken on so many dangerous missions...

Then he'd gotten the worst news of his life. His parents had been murdered in their own home. Ava had been the only witness, and she'd been shattered.

He drove away from the ranch, following behind Jamie.

Jamie. Now, that woman was a mystery to him. Beautiful, smart...

And...sometimes, I can see pain in her eyes. Pain and fear.

The same stark expression that he'd caught in his own sister's eyes. Jamie had a dark past, one that she hadn't shared with anyone. He knew the signs.

He also knew... *I don't want anyone to hurt her again.*

Jamie wasn't like other women. There was something different about her. Something that pulled at him. Something that called *to* him. Not just desire, though he sure felt plenty of lust for her.

The woman had made him laugh that night.

Since his parents' death, he hadn't exactly had a whole lot to laugh about. Jamie—she was just different.

He sped up a bit as he headed toward her place.

Whatever was waiting for Jamie, he wanted to be there with her. She might not be used to threats, but he was.

His truck ate up the miles. Her home was a little cottage nestled on two acres, a place that gave her plenty of privacy. When he pulled onto her lane, he didn't see the flash of police lights, and he knew they'd beat the cops there.

Jamie was already exiting her vehicle. Hurrying to the house.

Dammit. Davis jumped out. "Jamie, stop!" The burglar could still be inside the place.

Jamie whirled toward him. He stalked toward her. As he approached, he could easily hear the blare of her alarm and the frantic barking of a dog.

"You should wait for the cops."

Jamie looked over her shoulder. "I have to make sure it's not him."

Him? "Jamie?"

She pulled away. "You didn't need to come. I—I've got this."

Then she was rushing toward her house again. This time, he ran right with her. She unlocked her front door. Stopped that blaring alarm. A big brown dog ran forward, and when the dog saw Jamie, its loud barks gave way to softer cries as the animal pushed his head against her.

"It's okay, Jinx, I'm here."

Davis eased deeper into the house. He made sure to keep Jamie within his line of sight. Nothing looked disturbed. No furniture overturned. Nothing smashed. Nothing—

He saw the shattered glass on the floor. "The window." Davis headed toward it. "The guy probably thought he'd break the glass and unlock it. Then your alarm went off." He slanted a quick glance at Jinx. "And so did your dog."

Jamie had bent near the dog. She was stroking the animal's broad head. "Jinx is a great watchdog," she said. "He's—"

Jinx snarled and lunged away from her. He raced right out of the front door and into the night.

"Jinx!"

Davis was already running after him. "That great watchdog has a scent," Davis said. And that meant… *Is the burglar still here?* Now, that didn't make sense. The guy should have fled the scene as soon as the alarm went off. But…

Davis ran toward the woods on the right of Jamie's property. The dog was bounding up ahead, and Davis heard the growl of an engine in the air. A rumble... The distinct rumble of a motorcycle.

He is still here.

The burglar had been hiding in the dark... waiting for Jamie to return?

Davis lunged forward, following that sound because his instincts had just shot into overdrive. If the guy had been hanging around, then he'd had other plans—plans that involved Jamie. He'd nearly reached the trees when the light from the motorcycle flashed into him, momentarily blinding Davis.

He heard Jamie scream as that motorcycle came right at him. Davis lunged to the side, and the bike missed him by inches as it shot past him. He jumped right back to his feet, his eyes on that motorcycle. The rider wore a dark helmet, so he couldn't see the guy's face. The dog was running after the bike, but there was no way Jinx was going to catch him.

"Davis!" Jamie grabbed his arm. "Are you hurt? I'm so sorry!" Her hands flew over him. "I didn't mean to drag you into this! I'd never want for anyone else to be hurt, I—"

He caught her hands. The tumble of her words stopped. The growl of the motorcycle was a distant sound now. "What's going on, Jamie?"

"B-burglar."

He didn't buy that. Especially because that hitch in her voice had been a telling sign of a lie. "Want to try again?"

"Are you hurt?"

He shook his head. "Didn't even scratch me." The guy had been too intent on fleeing. His goal hadn't been to attack Davis. *So just what did the guy want?* "You said you didn't mean to drag me into this… What is this, Jamie? Tell me what's happening."

But she pulled away from him. Her arms wrapped around her stomach even as her shoulders hunched. Her dog rushed back to her side and pressed against her legs.

"Jamie?"

She looked toward her house. The lights blazed inside. The growl of the motorcycle was gone. And there was still no sign of the cops.

She's too isolated out here. What if she'd come back alone and that jerk had been waiting? His hands clenched as he thought of just what sick things the guy might have planned.

"You were nearly run down. That's what I meant." She backed up a step. "I shouldn't

have let you play Good Samaritan tonight.
I shouldn't—"

He reached out. Touched her arm. Felt the
tremble that shook through her. "Sweetheart,
sometimes, I can almost feel your secrets between us." Did she think he hadn't noticed
them?

She became very, very still. "You don't
want to know my secrets."

*Yes, I do. And I'm not going to stop dig-
ging until I uncover every single one of them.*

"I don't even want to know them." She
turned from him and headed toward her
house with slow, certain steps. "That's why I
spend most days pretending they don't exist."

She kept walking toward her house. Jinx
looked at Davis, whined, then hurried after
Jamie. Davis's gaze swept the scene once
more. Danger was out there, waiting to close
in on Jamie. And whatever trouble the woman
had stalking her...he wasn't going to leave
her to face it on her own.

Not alone. Not alone. Not alone!

His gloved fingers tightened around the
motorcycle's handlebars. Jamie should have
returned to that little house by herself. Some
hick in a pickup truck shouldn't have followed
her. He shouldn't have touched her.

He shouldn't have been with my Jamie!

When he heard the shriek of police sirens, he killed the lights on his motorcycle and took the ride off the road. He hid beneath some trees, watching as two cruisers rushed by. Those cars were heading to Jamie's place. Her house was the only one out on that long road.

He glanced at his watch. Hit the button for fast illumination. And he smiled when he saw the time. It had certainly taken the cops a long time to respond to that alarm. *If* Jamie had been alone, he would have been able to spend plenty of quality time with her before the police showed up. So much time. Time to catch up.

Time to punish.

He'd remember that for his next little visit to Jamie's place. Because he would be heading back there. Jamie wasn't slipping through his fingers. He'd found her, and he would never let her go again.

Chapter Two

"You don't have to stay here by yourself."

The cops had just left. They'd talked to Jamie. Searched her house and the edge of her property. They'd jotted down notes, and they hadn't seemed overly optimistic that her unwanted visitor would ever be identified.

"Just some kid...probably thinking he'd make an easy score." Those had been the words from one of the cops. He'd shrugged. Just *shrugged* while she stared at him in growing terror. She wanted the break-in to be some fluke. But...

I'm scared it isn't.

"Jamie, why don't you come out and stay at the ranch tonight?"

Her gaze jerked toward Davis. He'd stayed with her, all during the interview with the cops. He'd altered between anger and frustration, especially when the fresh-faced cops hadn't immediately phoned in the news about the guy on the motorcycle.

"There are plenty of rooms at the place," he said, voice low, easy. "I'm not asking you to share my bed."

She could feel her cheeks burn.

"I'm just offering you a safe place for the night. You can get the window repaired tomorrow, and then everything can return to normal for you."

Normal. What a fun word. "That's really not necessary." She tried to sound unruffled—as if she totally had this situation in hand. "I can board up the window tonight. I'll be fine here."

His green eyes seemed to darken a bit. "What if he comes back?"

"I have a gun." Okay, she'd blurted that bit. But it was Texas... Heck, most people had guns. She'd never used a gun in her life until she came down here, but...she'd just started feeling nervous in the past few weeks. Having bad dreams. So she'd gone to the shooting range. She'd learned to shoot pretty dang well during those visits.

His eyelids flickered. "Would you use it on someone?"

She didn't know. She hoped she'd never have to find out. Jinx padded into the den.

The dog glanced at her, then Davis, then he just sort of flopped down.

As was his way.

"I can't leave Jinx," she told him. "We'll both be fine here, really." Then she headed for the door. They'd had an amazing kiss and, then they'd gone to…this. A completely weird and uncomfortable situation in which he'd nearly been run down.

Story of my life. Bad things happen near me.

There was a reason she didn't let too many people get close to her. When people got close, they had a tendency to get hurt.

Or to wind up dead.

You'll never be happy, Jamie. Never. I won't let you go to another!

For an instant, that voice thundered through her mind. So strong and clear…as if the man who'd once shouted those words was actually standing there. Goose bumps rose on her arms.

Davis stalked toward her. She thought he'd just walk through the door and leave her to have a mini breakdown in peace. He didn't. He stopped right in front of her, gazed down at her and asked, "Do you think I don't know you're afraid?"

Were her knees knocking together that loudly?

"And it's not just tonight, is it? There's more…so much more." His fingers lifted toward her face, and she didn't mean to, but Jamie flinched.

He instantly froze. "Someone hurt you."

More than you can imagine. "Good night, Davis. Thanks for following me home. And I'm…I'm so sorry for all the trouble."

Anger flashed in his eyes. She almost took a step back. Almost. Then she remembered. He was one of the good guys.

"Don't apologize to me. I should have stopped the jerk. I didn't. I'm the one who needs to say that I'm sorry." His lips thinned. "And I am… I'm sorry that I didn't give chase right then, but I didn't want to leave you. I didn't know if anyone else might still be lurking around, and I didn't want to take a chance, not when I didn't realize what was happening."

Her breath felt cold in her lungs.

"Why don't you tell me what's happening? Because I know you're spooked."

"My house was broken into… Anyone would be spooked from that."

He waited.

"Good night," she said again.

He sighed. Then he snapped his fingers together. "Jinx." His voice was low, commanding, and her dog instantly bounded to his feet.

She frowned at the dog. He usually only listened to her. Half the time.

"I'll put your dog in my truck. You get an overnight bag."

Wait, what?

"You're scared, so the way I see it...there are two choices. I can stay here with you... or you can come back to the ranch with me."

She didn't want to be in her house. It was odd because she loved the place, but...everywhere she looked, Jamie saw a threat. *Too isolated.* She'd enjoyed the privacy before, but now she thought...*he can watch me from anyplace.*

"The ranch is huge—you'll have plenty of privacy, and if you come back with me, I'll actually be able to sleep tonight. I won't stay up, worrying about you every second."

His words had her lips curving. "I don't think you'd worry that much."

His gaze was on her mouth, and his eyes seemed to be heating. "Yes...I would."

Tension was between them. Heavy. A bit hot.

"Come home with me," Davis said.

And...she nodded.

HE'D NEVER ASKED a woman to spend the night at the ranch. The ranch was home, it was family. His twin brother, Brodie, lived there with his wife, Jennifer, and Davis had actually been thinking it was time he found a new place…so he could give those two privacy. Before Jennifer had rolled back into Brodie's life, it had just been Davis and his twin out at the ranch. The rest of their family had stayed away because the place held too many painful memories.

Ava, in particular, had hated the ranch. When she'd looked at the place, he knew she didn't see the good times. She just saw blood and death.

But that's changing. We're making new memories now. Seeing good…and not just the bad.

"Looks like the party finally ended," Jamie said as she stood by her car. She'd followed him back to his home. He'd offered to just drive her, but Jamie had been adamant that she'd wanted her own transportation. "All of the cars are gone."

They'd talked to the cops for a while at her place. Not that those uniforms had been much help. They hadn't even wanted to put out an APB for the motorcycle. So, while the cops had asked aimless questions again and again, the perp had gotten away.

And he'd better not come back.

"It's after midnight now," Davis said as he glanced around. "I guess the party had to end sometime." Though he still had trouble believing that his baby sister was actually married. Sweet Ava, all grown up.

"I guess it did." She opened her car's back door, and Jinx bounded out to stand at her side. Before she could grab her bag, Davis leaned in and took it. When he pulled back, Jamie's gaze was on him. "How am I supposed to thank you for this?"

Oh, I can come up with some ways. But he was playing the gentleman, so he bit those words back. He didn't want to make Jamie any more nervous than she already was. And coming on to her too strong, well…

After that kiss, she already knows how much I want her. He'd nearly jumped her right beneath that tree, with all the wedding guests just yards away. Davis had thought about kissing Jamie plenty of times. He'd wondered how she'd taste. He'd never thought his lips would touch hers and his control would incinerate.

It had.

A one-time fluke…or a sign of an addiction to come?

He carried her bag toward the guesthouse. "The place is plenty pet friendly, so Jinx can go inside and get settled for the night." Since the guesthouse was privately positioned away from the main ranch, he'd thought she might feel more comfortable there. The ranch had top-of-the-line security, so Jamie would be safe for the night. He unlocked the door for her and turned off the alarm. He motioned for her to enter, but Jamie hesitated. Jinx didn't. The dog hurried inside and then—flopped near the door.

"I, um, thank you." She pushed back the hair that had fallen over her cheek. "It's really nice of you to let me stay like this. I mean, you barely know me and—"

"I know plenty about you."

Her breath caught. She searched his eyes, then her shoulders slumped a bit. "Ah, you *think* you do." And she crossed the threshold and entered the guesthouse. "We always think we know someone, but it's all surface. All what we want someone else to see."

Before she'd left her house, Jamie had changed into a pair of jeans and a loose shirt. He couldn't help but notice how well those jeans hugged her curves.

Eyes up. Clearing his throat, he focused on her face once more. She was watching him, her head tilted to the side.

"What's beneath your surface?" Davis asked her, truly curious now. Why did Jamie seem to hold herself back from so many people? He knew there had been plenty of guys who were interested in the doc, only she hadn't been interested in them. He'd actually thought she'd shoot him down, too, but then she'd kissed him so wildly, so recklessly beneath the branches of that tree.

"You don't want to know." Jamie exhaled on a faint sigh. "Thank you, again."

Ah, so she was trying to kick him out. Right. He gave her a little salute and backed up. "If you should get scared, just press one on the alarm panel. I can be here in a moment."

Jamie nodded. "I'll remember that."

He hesitated. "Are we going to talk about it?"

Her cheeks flushed. "You mean—"

"The kiss that left me aching for you."

That light flush became even darker. She was so cute when she blushed.

"If that alarm call hadn't come through, what do you think would have happened next?" Davis asked, curious. He knew what he'd *wanted* to happen but...

"I would have told you good-night. The same way I'm doing now."

His lips quirked. He turned away from her. *Shot down.*

"Davis, you don't want the trouble I bring."

Her low words had him glancing back at her. "I can handle trouble. It's kind of my specialty."

She swallowed. "You and your family… you're good guys, and I wanted to—"

She'd done it again. Made him laugh. The sound was rusty even to his own ears. "Oh, sweetheart," he finally managed. "Whatever made you think I was one of the good guys?"

Jamie took a step back. "But…"

"Let's be clear. I want you like damn hell on fire right now. I've been fantasizing about you for months. When I finally got my hands on you tonight…well, the desire I felt just got stronger. I want you." Davis stared straight into her eyes as he said these words because he wanted to be very clear on this point. "But don't mistake me for some good, easygoing kind of guy. That's not who I am." He was the kind of guy who saw what he wanted and took it.

He didn't play by the rules, and he sure wasn't afraid of any danger. In fact, he thrived on adrenaline.

"But how do you feel, Jamie?" Because

he needed to know. He closed the space between them. If the woman didn't want him, if he'd imagined the fire of her response, then he'd back off. Sure, they'd touched, and he'd thought the world had exploded; but maybe she hadn't felt that way, maybe...

"I didn't expect the way I feel." Her gaze dropped. Her long lashes shielded her eyes, so he couldn't read the emotions there. "Maybe because I've tried not to feel anything in so long."

I'm going to discover all your secrets, Jamie. She was a puzzle to him, one that he would be solving very, very soon.

He caught her chin between his thumb and forefinger and gently pushed her head up, so that she was staring into his eyes once again.

"I want you, too," she whispered. "But it's so fast. I don't want to make a mistake."

Fast...she must not have realized he'd been lusting after her for the past year. That whenever he knew she was coming to the McGuire ranch, he'd made sure that he was there, too. That if he caught sight of her in town, he dropped everything else to go and get close to her. Accidental meetings? Right.

He'd played things cool for too long. Time to turn up the heat.

"It won't be a mistake." He leaned toward

her. Their lips were barely an inch apart. "It will be incredible." Then he kissed her. Not the deep, consuming kiss that he wanted. But a light, soft good-night kiss. A tease for what was to come…because there would be plenty coming for them. She wanted him, and he'd use that. In the end, they'd both get what they desired.

"Good night, Jamie." He smiled at her. "Sweet dreams." Then he walked away before he gave in to his baser urges and did a whole lot more than just kiss her good-night.

JAMIE SHUT THE door behind Davis. She turned around, leaned her back against the wood, and her fingers touched her lips. She could still feel him. The warm, soft press of his mouth on hers.

It had been so long since she'd let anyone get close to her. There'd been no lovers, not in years. Because it was far too dangerous to trust a man on that level. Dangerous for her.

Dangerous for him.

But…

Sweet dreams.

But a woman could sure dream.

JAMIE HADN'T RETURNED HOME.

The motorcycle idled between his legs as

he stared at her dark house. He'd gone back, sure that she'd be there, all alone and waiting.

But her car wasn't there. No cars were there. The house sat, shadowy and silent...

Where are you, Jamie?

He turned off the motorcycle. Strode toward the house. This time, he was careful. He'd come prepared. It only took a few minutes to disable her alarm. Then he went back to the window he'd broken before. Someone had nailed a board over it. Probably that hick who'd been in the truck. The one who never should have been near Jamie.

As if the board will stop me.

He just broke another window. The glass shattered and—

Silence.

No alarm. No shrieking dog. But also... no Jamie.

Where are you, love?

He lifted the window and climbed inside. The room was dark, but he could smell Jamie there. Light lavender. He'd never forgotten that scent, not in all the long years that had passed. He could almost feel her in the house.

He turned on the lights. Saw that he was in her den. Everything was neat. Put in its place. Same Jamie. She'd always been so organized. She had shelves filled with books. Paintings lined the walls. Paintings that he knew she'd done. She'd always had talent. A lifetime ago, she'd made sketches of him. She sketched her family. Her home. Everything.

There were no personal sketches, though. Not even any photos. No family mementos that he could see.

He stalked through the house. Cookbooks in the kitchen. Pots, pans…nothing personal.

He went into her bedroom. Her scent was stronger there. Her bed was made, a tidy four-poster of dark cherrywood. He opened the drawers of her dresser. Touched her soft silken gowns. Opened another drawer. Saw her bras. Lacy. Beautiful. Scraps of sexy underwear.

She'd better not be wearing these for anyone else.

His fingers clenched around the gown in his left hand. He'd told Jamie, so long ago, that she would always be his. They were linked, and nothing—no one—would ever tear them apart.

Not even Jamie.

He didn't forgive her for what she'd done. Forgiveness wouldn't come easily, but they would get past this dark patch. After Jamie had been punished, they could start building their life again.

He threw down the gown and headed for her little nightstand. There, finally, was a picture. Jamie was in that picture, smiling up at him.

But Jamie wasn't alone. He recognized the man with her. The man who had his arm so casually wrapped around Jamie. The fool who was smiling at the camera.

The dead man.

His fist slammed into that frame, punching at the glass. He'd cut himself when he busted the window earlier, and his blood dripped onto the photo.

He was staring down at the man who'd made Jamie hate him, the man who'd made her turn away all of those years ago. Jamie still had a picture of *him*?

No, no, this wouldn't work. Time for her punishment to begin right then.

He took the photo. Shoved it into his pocket. Then his gaze darted around her house. This wasn't Jamie's real home. She needed to see that. This place was nothing but an illusion... an illusion that would...

Go up in smoke.

"JAMIE, JAMIE, RUN!"

She stared in horror at the scene before her.

"He's got a gun, run!"

But she couldn't run. She was rooted to the spot, and when the gunshot blasted, she screamed. Screamed again and again and—

Jamie jerked up in bed, her heart racing as the dream slowly faded from her mind.

Sweet dreams. Her fingers clenched around the covers. Right. As if she ever had those. Instead, memories from her past plagued her, haunting her and never letting go. No matter how hard she tried, she just couldn't escape from them.

She rose from the bed. She could see the faint light of dawn streaking toward her, cracking through the blinds. Another night had passed. The day would be better. It had to be.

That was her mantra, anyway. The way she got through all the dark nights of her life.

The day would be better. It had to be.

It was Sunday, so her clinic wasn't open. She didn't have to rush in to check on her four-legged friends.

Jinx brushed against her leg. She bent down, her fingers pushing against his fur. "It's okay. You know the drill. Sleep means the nightmares come back." After so much time, she'd thought those dreams would fade. But then, maybe some memories never vanished.

A sharp rap at the front door had her tensing.

The knock came again, harder. "Jamie!"

She hurried from the bedroom and toward the main door. That was Davis's voice—she'd recognize it anywhere. Most people confused Davis and Brodie, but she didn't. She saw all the small differences between them. The way Davis's eyes crinkled a bit more at the corners, the way his voice was a shade deeper, the way—

"Jamie!"

She fumbled with the locks and opened the door. She'd slept in her clothes, too nervous to change last night.

"We've got a problem," Davis said, his voice grim. As grim as the expression on his face. The faint lines near his eyes had sharpened.

"Problem?"

Sympathy flashed in his eyes. "It's your house. Someone saw the smoke this morning and called the fire department. It's just... It caught fire, Jamie. Your place burned last night."

IT WAS GONE. The entire house was just a blackened shell now. Jamie stood in front of her home, watching as the firefighters examined the smoldering rubble.

"The alarm should have gone off," she said,

feeling numb. *Gone.* Everything was destroyed. The bitter scent of ash filled the air, and Jamie found herself shaking her head, desperate for *this* to be just a bad dream. That home…she'd tried so hard to make it hers. She'd planted flowers around her windows. She and Jinx had spent hours outside, chasing balls, playing.

"I checked with your alarm company," Davis said. He was at her side. Just as he'd been, ever since they'd arrived at this nightmare scene. "They never got any sort of signal from your place. I'll do some investigating, but my hunch is that your alarm was cut."

Her gaze swung to Davis. "Cut? You're saying that you think someone did this? It was no accident?"

"I was with you when you packed up. I saw you double-check the stove, the heater…everything was safe. The fire marshal will be able to tell us the cause once he investigates fully, but, for the place to go up like this—" his right hand gestured back to the blackened house "—and for the alarm not to go off, right after some jerk tried to break in to your place…" His lips thinned. "No, my gut is sure saying it wasn't an accident."

And her gut clenched painfully.

"He probably came back later, once he

thought the coast was clear. Maybe he set the fire to cover up the robbery. The guy could have thought he'd cover his tracks that way."

She'd had a TV in there, not one that was top of the line, but still a good TV. A computer, a DVD player, an e-reader. It *could* have been a robbery.

Jamie shivered. Or it could have been something else.

Has he found me? It had been so long. She'd thought she was safe. No, she'd just hoped that she was.

"Jamie?" Davis brushed his fingers over her arm. "Is there something you aren't telling me?"

She didn't trust others easily. After what she'd been through, Jamie knew that trust was a mistake but… *Should I tell him?*

She just didn't know. Jamie straightened her shoulders. "Excuse me, I want to go and talk with the fire marshal."

She wanted to see if there was anything at all that could be salvaged from the wreckage. Or if she'd just lost every bit of her home. She hurried forward and…

A photo was on the ground. Not near the house. Not burned by the fire. Just lying there.

Jamie bent and picked it up. The sunlight

poured down on her, so she could easily see the image. Her. Smiling. Happy. So long ago.

Jamie shoved the photo into her pocket even as she tried to blink away tears. That photo shouldn't have been outside. She'd put it on her nightstand. The photo was the only thing she'd brought from her old life. It should have been in the house. It wasn't worth stealing. It wasn't…

I don't think someone came to rob me. I think someone came to hurt me.

And if that was the case, then she was going to have to tell Davis. She'd have to tell him the darkest secrets of her life.

Chapter Three

Jamie was back at the McGuire ranch, and this time, she wasn't there for some sort of celebration. She'd lost nearly everything she owned—everything but the overnight bag she'd brought with her when she'd slept at the guesthouse. Everything else had been gone in an instant.

"You'll stay with me," Davis said as he paced in front of her. They were at the main house, not the guesthouse. He'd brought her back there after she'd spent hours staring at the wreckage of her home, looking for answers. Finding none. "You'll be safe here and—"

"I can afford a hotel room, you know." She stood a few feet away from him, her hands at her sides. "And I've got insurance on the house. I'll be fine, really."

Silence.

Jamie glanced over and met Davis's stare.

Do it. "But there is something I need." The reason she'd agreed to travel back to the ranch with him. So they could talk. Alone. She braced herself because she *hated* going back to her past. There just didn't seem to be a choice right then. "I want to hire you."

His dark brows rose.

"Everyone in the area knows just how good the McGuire Securities firm is." She'd learned all of the background on their PI business long ago. When the cops hadn't succeeded in finding their parents' killers, Davis and his brothers had formed their own private investigation firm. They'd been making a name for themselves not just in Texas, but in the entire South and along the East Coast, as well. Each of the McGuire brothers had served in the military, and they were putting that training to use in a different capacity—hunting, privately. Hunting killers. Stalkers.

She could sure use his deadly skills right then.

"The police are going to search for the robber." He spoke slowly. "I know you probably don't have much faith in those uniforms, but—"

"You were right," Jamie said, cutting him off. "I do have secrets. And I need to make sure that one of those secrets isn't coming back to hurt me." *Again.* During the ride back to his place, she'd weighed her options. She'd tried to think of alternatives, but she didn't have many.

Davis. He's my best bet.

He walked toward her. His steps were slow, oddly graceful. Kind of like a big jungle cat, stalking his prey.

"If it's just a robber, some guy who torched my place because he didn't want to leave fingerprints behind…" She laughed and the sound was bitter. "I'd be grateful for that."

She and Davis were alone in the house. Jamie had caught sight of his twin when they'd arrived—Brodie had been at the stables. She hadn't wanted to share this story with anyone but Davis. Just telling him was hard enough.

But I have to be sure. I have to know…

"I wasn't always Jamie Myers," she said. "I used to be someone else. Someone with an entirely different life. My name was Jamie Bridgeton."

He didn't speak. Didn't push her. Just stared. Waited.

She bit her lower lip. She'd never told anyone else this story. "I made a mistake—a long time ago. The worst mistake I'd ever made. That mistake cost me the life I'd known."

"What did you do?"

There was no judgment from him. But then, he didn't understand.

"I trusted the wrong man. Fell in love with the wrong boy. Henry Westport." But he'd seemed so perfect. She'd known him for years. Gone to school with him. Grown up with him. She should have seen the darkness in him, but...

She hadn't. Not until it was too late.

"I was seventeen when it happened." She turned away from him because Jamie didn't want to look in Davis's eyes when she told him this. The pain was still too raw. "Seventeen when I realized that he was being too controlling. That he was trying to cut everyone else out of my life. Seventeen when I told him goodbye, for the first time." Her hand lifted and rubbed against her side. The wound didn't hurt. None of the wounds hurt, not anymore. But they were still there, silent reminders.

They always would be.

"I broke up with him." It was easier to talk without looking at Davis. And she could *almost* imagine that the story she was telling was about someone else. Another girl. *Not me. That couldn't have happened to me.* "I ended things with him, and the next day...

he broke into my bedroom. He stabbed me six times."

"What?"

There was such fury in that one word, such desperate fury that she spun around. Davis hadn't moved. Not so much as a step, but his eyes glittered with his rage.

"The police arrested him. I got stitched up." She paused, recalling those drug-filled hours in the hospital. "I thought it was over." A nightmare, gone. "But…" This was the part that shamed her. That hurt her. "But my father's business had recently suffered a… rather substantial loss. And Henry's dad, he was quite wealthy. I didn't even realize the deal had been struck, not at first." Maybe she hadn't wanted to believe it. "But suddenly, the DA was saying that Henry would get counseling. He was only seventeen, too, see… he was actually a few months younger than me. He was going to get counseling because he was so troubled. Troubled…" She repeated the word, frowning a bit now, as she had then. *Troubled* just didn't seem to cover things for her. *Troubled…* He'd broken into her house. Stabbed her as he screamed that no one else could have her. That she was meant to be with him. That she'd always see that.

I'll make you see, Jamie!

If her brother hadn't burst into the room, Henry would have killed her.

She swallowed. "Weeks later, I found out that my father had gotten a rather substantial settlement from Henry's family. Not a pay-off—my father assured me it wasn't a pay-off. He said he talked with the DA and agreed to a plea because it was in my best interest. I mean...why go to court? Why subject myself to a nasty trial?" Her father's words felt unnatural coming out of her mouth. "Henry was obviously sick, so he should get treatment. I should move on...college waited. The future waited." He'd said those things to her, and they had been like nails, driving beneath her skin. *No, not nails. Like Henry's knife.* She'd been numb when her father talked to her. Numb. Jamie remembered asking one thing... *When will he get out, Dad?*

Her father hadn't told her.

Later, she'd learned it didn't matter.

"What happened next?" Davis's voice was so rough that she flinched. He exhaled on a hard sigh. "I didn't mean... Jamie, look at me."

She did.

"Do you trust me?"

I trusted the wrong man before.

"Because I think you do. I think that's why you're telling me this story."

She shook her head. "I don't actually trust anyone." She didn't make that mistake. "But I need to hire you. I need to know…" *Tell him the rest.* "Henry came after me again. Months later. I was just about to start college, and he found me."

Davis was still staring into her eyes.

"He had a gun this time." Her hand slid into her pocket. Closed around the picture there. A picture of her and her brother. "My brother, Warren, was there with me. He fought Henry. Told me to run, but I—I couldn't just leave my brother. I loved him." So she'd stayed. She'd grabbed for that gun.

"Henry shot my brother. He was going to shoot me." Her breath chilled her lungs. "But the campus police arrived. They took him away. By the time he was even at lockup, his parents were there, talking about his psychotic break. Saying they'd get him the best therapy. That he'd be better." She pulled out the photo. Stared at the image of her brother. "My brother was on an operating room table, fighting for his life."

Davis reached out and took the picture from her.

"I went to the police station. I wanted to

make sure Henry didn't just get *therapy* this time." She licked lips that had gone so dry. "He told me…screamed at me…that I wouldn't get away from him. That he'd find a way to keep me. That he'd kill anyone who came between us, the same way he'd killed my brother."

The pain clawed through her, tearing at her insides. There was a very good reason why she didn't talk about the past. It hurt far too much.

"Jamie?"

"My brother never made it off the operating room table. He died protecting me, and Henry was there at the police station, screaming that everyone else I loved would die, too. That he wasn't going to stop. That he'd keep coming…" Her shoulders straightened.

"They locked him up?" Davis demanded. His voice was a rough growl.

"Psychotic break. All the shrinks agreed that he'd suffered one." *Jail isn't the right place for my son.* How many times had Garrison Westport said those words? "He was confined to a psychiatric facility—maximum security."

I wanted to feel safe then. I tried…but it didn't work. Jamie bit her lip, not wanting to tell him of the betrayal that followed. Maybe Davis didn't need to know that part, not yet.

So she glossed over it. "I couldn't stay there forever. Sooner or later, he'd get out, and he'd come for me."

That had been her fear. That she'd wake up again and find him standing over her, the knife gripped in his hand. "So I...I left. The US Marshals helped me. Maybe they just took pity on me. But I got set up with a new last name. A new life. And I thought that maybe I could be safe." *And that Henry would leave everyone else alone.*

He shook his head. "You've been carrying all of this on your shoulders?"

"I would have kept carrying it, but that photo in your hand...it was on my night-stand. Framed. Somehow that photo escaped the flames."

A muscle flexed in his jaw. "You think it's a message."

"I'm scared he's found me again. I—I need you to dig for me. That's what you do, right? Dig for the truth? Please, I'll pay anything, I just— I need to know if Henry has come for me again. I need to know if I have to run again. If I—"

He caught her hand in his. "You aren't running."

Easy for him to say. He didn't have this particular demon on his trail.

"I'll find out what's happening," Davis vowed, "but promise you won't run."

That wasn't a promise she could make.

And, obviously, he must have read that truth on her face because Davis said, "Give me a few days. Let me figure out what's happening."

"A few days." That was all she'd agree to right then. Because if Henry was in the area, if he'd managed to find her again...

She would run as far as necessary.

"AND THAT'S HER STORY," Davis said as he propped his back against the wall and stared at his brothers. Brodie let out a low whistle while Sullivan, the youngest brother in the family, just shook his head.

"She wants us to find out who set that fire," Davis continued. "And I told her we'd take the case."

Sullivan rolled back his shoulders. "It *could* have just been some punk trying to cover his tracks after he robbed the place. I mean, that picture could have just blown out during the commotion. We don't know it's that guy from her past, Henry—"

"Henry Westport."

"We don't know it's him yet. And if it's not, we sure don't want to do anything to tip the guy off to Jamie's current location," Sullivan added as his gaze turned contemplative. "If the guy has moved on, the last thing you want is him to suddenly get fixated on her again. Before we move in on him, I'll do some digging. See what I can find out about the man and his recent movements. If he's in the area, I'll have that info within twenty-four hours."

He'd known that he could count on his brothers. Always.

"She'll stay here until then," Brodie said, nodding as if that were a given. "With the new security enhancements we put in, this is the best place for her."

Damn straight. She'd mentioned going to a hotel. His first thought on that had been... *hell, no.* She'd be far too exposed at one of the local hotels. Davis needed her close by, so that he could keep an eye on her. He just— *I need her close.*

"Is there anything else we need to know about this case?" Sullivan asked as he strolled toward the window and peered out.

"I've told you everything she said to me."

Sullivan kept staring out the window. What was he looking at? Frowning, Davis crossed the room until he was at his brother's side. Then he looked through the window and saw Jamie. She was standing near the stables. The light hit her hair, turning it even brighter as it tumbled over her shoulders.

"She's a beautiful woman," Sullivan said simply.

Davis's jaw locked. His gaze cut to Sullivan. Yes, he recognized that heat in his blood for the jealousy that it was. *Back off, brother.*

"I'm just wondering..." Sullivan murmured. "If this case might be personal." He jerked his thumb toward a silent Brodie. "Lately, I swear you guys have a tendency to make every damn case we take personal. I turn around, and someone's in love or getting hitched. It's starting to make me twitchy."

"Jerk," Brodie tossed out. "Jennifer and I were involved long before her case. I just didn't tell you that because I'm not the kiss-and-tell type."

Sullivan smirked. "Right."

Brodie's eyes narrowed.

Sullivan didn't look as if he cared about the white-hot glare Brodie was sending his way. He glanced back at Davis. "So I'm just curious. Is this a strictly business case or is it more?"

Davis thought about the way Jamie had felt when they'd kissed. How perfectly she'd fit into his arms. Then he thought about the rage that had ignited inside of him when he'd heard about her past. "It's more."

Sullivan's jaw dropped. "*What?* No, man, hell, no, I was just ragging on you! I was just—"

"She's a friend to this family. There's no way this is just business with a friend." But he wanted Jamie to be more than a friend. How much more, well, that remained to be seen. Now that he knew about her past, he'd have to tread carefully. The last thing he wanted to do was frighten her but...

I've been standing in the shadows too long. Watching, waiting for the perfect moment to approach her. But every time he'd gotten close in the past, he'd been tongue-tied when he neared her. Hell, he usually had a line ready for anyone or anything. But when Jamie looked at him with her big, blue eyes, he got a little lost.

I am in such trouble.

"Friend..." Sullivan drew that one word out until it seemed to stretch for three syllables. "Not lover?"

Now Davis was glaring at him. "Just work the case. Just—"

"This is about the case," Sullivan fired back. Sullivan "Sully" was an ex-marine. And though he was the youngest brother, lately

Davis had started to realize that the guy had the hardest edge in the family. The deaths of their parents had completely altered Sully. A dark intensity seemed to cling to him like a second skin. "If you're involved with a woman who happens to have a psychotic ex, what do you think that does to you?" His eyes sharpened. "It makes you a target. It makes you a man in that guy's way."

If it meant that he'd be keeping Jamie safe, then Davis would gladly step right into her stalker's path.

"Are you sleeping with her?" Sullivan asked bluntly.

Davis lunged for the guy. Others might be afraid of Sullivan, but he never would be. Sully was still his younger brother, even if they were the same height, and Sullivan had about fifteen pounds on him. So Davis grabbed the guy and shoved him against the nearest wall. "Respect," he gritted out. "That woman has been through hell. You will treat her with respect. I know you're going through something right now—something you're not telling any of us."

Sullivan's gaze cut away.

Did you think I didn't know?

"But you need to watch yourself. Brother or no brother, I will take you down. Jamie is scared. She's on an emotional tightrope, and I won't have you doing anything to upset her."

Sullivan inclined his head. "Understood."

Davis let him go and watched as Sullivan straightened his shirt. Then, he just had to ask, "What is going on with you, man? I feel as if you're sliding away from us." Sullivan seemed so tense, so angry all the time lately.

Sullivan's lips curled in a twisted smile. "What? Like you two have a monopoly on things getting personal? Everyone else is happy, they're all moving on...but none of you even know what I lost."

What? Davis glanced over at Brodie. His twin looked as clueless as he felt.

"Forget it," Sullivan muttered, and he walked past Davis. "She's forgotten me, so it's all good." He straightened his shoulders. "I'll dig into Henry Westport's life. If he's been within a two hundred mile radius of Austin, you'll know. Until then...well, keep your woman out of the fire."

And then Sullivan was gone. He headed for the front door. He closed it softly behind him. Sullivan rarely stayed overnight at the ranch. Because of their parents? Or something else? *Someone* else?

"What in the hell was that about?" Brodie asked.

Davis shook his head. "I thought you would know."

"No clue." Brodie's green gaze—a gaze all the McGuire brothers shared—turned pensive. "But you can bet I'll be finding out. And if I can't get him to talk, I'll send in the big guns."

The big guns...that would be Ava. Because none of the brothers could resist her. Davis often thought that, of all the McGuires, Ava was actually the strongest, even if she looked the most delicate. That woman had walked through fire, but she'd come out tougher. More determined than ever to be happy with her life.

And not let the shadows of the past drag her down.

For years, people in the area had whispered about Ava. Some had even thought that she'd been involved in the murder of her parents. Davis had known that talk was bull, and he'd gotten into more fights than he could count when some fool had repeated that poison gossip near him.

Now, finally, they were getting more clues to lead them to the real identity of the killers. Two men who'd attacked their parents so brutally, first shooting and killing Davis's mother, then turning the weapon on his father.

"I'll never tell you. No matter what you do. I'll never tell."

Ava had told them those had been their father's words as he'd faced the gunmen.

"What are you holding back?" Brodie asked him.

Davis had returned to the window. He was staring out, at Jamie. "I think she might be a lot like Ava." Delicate on the outside, but a core of pure steel on the inside. "I don't want to see her hurt." He could reveal more with Brodie. Not that he could ever hide much from the guy, anyway. Brodie was too in sync with him.

He and Brodie—their link went deep. They watched over each other, always. Davis had even become a SEAL because he'd wanted to make sure he was out there to watch his brother's back. He was older than Brodie by five minutes—that meant something, right? *It's my job to keep him alive.*

Brodie's hand clapped over his shoulder. "We'll keep her safe."

Davis nodded.

"We got Jennifer through the danger," Brodie said, speaking of his now wife. A woman who'd burst into their lives with plenty of secrets—and a truckload full of danger following behind her. "We'll protect Jamie, too."

Right, they—

Jamie was running toward the house. Instantly, Davis tensed, and then he was rushing for the front door. He yanked it open just as Jamie reached the threshold. Her cheeks were flushed, her eyes shining with worry.

"What is it?" Davis demanded immediately as he reached out and pulled her close. "What happened?" His body went into battle-ready alertness.

"My answering service called... I have to get out to the Hollows' ranch right away. Their mare went into labor." She shook her head. "It's way too early. Shade isn't supposed to have that foal for weeks. I have to get out there, *now*." She pulled away from him. "I'll be out there until the danger has passed. I just... I wanted to tell you before I left."

Jamie turned her back on him and hurried down the stairs. "I'll stop by my clinic and grab supplies," she called over her shoulder. "Then I'll be at the Hollows' ranch. If you need me—"

Davis ran after her and beat her to her car. "Sweetheart, I'm coming with you."

Her eyes widened in surprise. He didn't know if the surprise came from the fact that he'd just slipped up—again—and called her sweetheart or if she was shocked that he would be going with her.

"Until I know more about what's happening," he told her quietly, "I'd feel better if I could keep an eye on you."

She swallowed, a delicate movement of her throat. "You think…he could really be here?"

"I don't know what's happening yet." A fine tension had slid over her. Making her lips quiver. Making her eyes go wider. He hated that he'd scared her, but he wanted Jamie to be on guard, at all times. "I don't know, but I won't risk you. Let me come with you, Jamie. I won't get in the way." *But I will keep you safe.*

She nodded.

"And let's take my truck. It will make better time over those rough roads." He tossed a quick wave to Brodie—his brother had followed them onto the porch—then Davis opened the truck door for Jamie. Moments later, they were rushing away from the Mc-Guire ranch.

HE KNEW THAT Jamie had always loved animals. Loved them far too much.

Once, she'd had a big, stray mutt of a dog

that she loved. Kind of like that hound she now kept. She'd called the old stray Lucy.

Lucy had gone everywhere with her.

And then one day, Lucy had vanished. She'd cried in his arm when Lucy disappeared. She'd hunted for hours for that dog. She'd put up posters. She'd searched.

But Lucy had never come home.

She couldn't come home. He'd hit the dog when it rushed in front of his car. Dented the damn fender.

The animals were a weakness for Jamie. Always had been, always would be.

He tapped the disposable cell phone against his steering wheel and stared at the darkened clinic. *Come on, Jamie...come out and see me...*

Because he'd sure been waiting to see her.

The minutes slid by, and he didn't move. He kept his gaze on the clinic. Kept waiting. And then...

Then he saw a truck slide into the parking lot. He smiled when Jamie jumped out of the vehicle and raced inside. His hand reached for the door handle on his left. He wasn't on the motorcycle this time. He'd taken this car—getting it had been so easy. He needed it so that he could take Jamie with him—

Jamie isn't alone.

The man who'd been at her house before—
the tall, dark-haired man, was hurrying after
her. Walking too close. Touching the small
of her back.

His fingers fisted.

Jamie had a new lover. He could tell by the
way the man touched Jamie. Possessive. Protective. *The way I should touch her!*

He'd told her once, they were meant to be
together forever. He wasn't going to let her go.

But he would get rid of that fool in his way.
*Jamie doesn't belong to you. She's mine. Al-
ways...mine.* He'd gone too long without
being close to Jamie, and in that time, she'd
turned to another.

No, no, that just wouldn't do.

Jamie rushed back out of the clinic, her bag
in her hand. The man was still at her side.

They jumped into the truck and rushed
away.

You don't get to run. I've got you now.

Chapter Four

"But I don't understand." Jamie frowned at Stephanie Hollow. "My answering service called. They said your foreman had telephoned, frantic. Shade was in labor and you needed me."

Stephanie shook her head and tucked a strand of red hair behind her ear. "No, we're okay out here. Shade's doing just fine." Her warm brown eyes showed her confusion. "I don't know what's happening, but that call didn't come from us. The foreman isn't even here today. He went back to Colorado to visit his family."

Davis's muscles had hardened with tension. The Hollow ranch was isolated, and they'd taken plenty of long, twisting turns to get out to the place. To get out there…for no apparent reason…

Except someone wanted Jamie here. Someone wanted to draw her out.

"Well, if something does happen—" Jamie inclined her head toward Stephanie "—just give me a call. You know I'll come right out."

Stephanie nodded, but she still looked worried. "I'm so sorry this happened. I hate you came all the way out here." Her gaze slid to Davis. "Uh, both of you. I didn't realize you two were, um, dating."

"Oh, we're not—" Jamie began.

Davis wrapped his arm around her shoulders. "We're not sorry we came out. Better to be safe than sorry, right, Jamie? Good seeing you, Stephanie." He steered Jamie back to the truck. He opened the door and let her slide into the passenger side.

"What are you doing?" Jamie demanded. "Now Stephanie is going to tell everyone we're involved!"

He hurried around the truck, jumped inside and quickly had the engine growling to life. "Sweetheart..." The endearment just flowed from him again, and he wasn't the type to use endearments casually. Never had been. "We've got bigger problems than some gossip." He headed down the graveled drive. "And if people want to think we're involved, good. That gives me a reason to stay close to you without folks knowing you've hired me and my brothers." Because he knew she wanted to keep her past secret.

"Bigger problems..." Her voice trailed away, and, from the corner of his eye, he saw her fingers clench around her bag. "You think... You think this wasn't a mix-up?"

"Get your service on the line," he told her. "Verify the information." But, no, he didn't think this was some service mix-up. Davis thought that she'd been lured out there. Lured out into the open.

Were you at the clinic? Did you think she'd arrive alone, but then I showed up, too?

His hands tightened around the wheel. Jamie had her phone out, and she was talking with her service. "Yes, yes, the Hollows' ranch. Stephanie said no one from the ranch called."

Silence.

"Are you sure about those details? All right, yes, thank you."

She sighed softly as she ended the call. "She confirmed the details. Said the caller identified himself as the foreman, and he *said* that Shade was in labor. I mean...how would someone know that? If it's Henry, how would he know—"

"You had a computer at your house, right?"

"Yes. A laptop."

"I'm guessing it contained patient files. He got the laptop, and he got all the information he needed. He knows your routine now. Your patient list. Whatever information you had on that laptop, he has now. And he can use it against you."

"You...you really think it's Henry."

"At this point, I don't have any reason to think it's someone else." He slanted a quick glance her way. "Unless there's something else in your past that you need to tell me about."

Her lips parted. "I... No. *No*."

There *was* something there. He could hear it in her voice. "Jamie, if there is something else I need to know about, another threat against you, then you need to tell me, now."

Her head turned toward him. "There's— *Look out!*"

But her scream came too late. Because another vehicle had just shot toward them. The driver had been hiding on the side of the road, right around the twisting curve. The vehicle roared forward and drove into the driver's side of the truck. The impact was bone-jarring. The crunch of metal and breaking glass filled the air even as the truck started to flip. The side air bag shot out, enveloping Davis in a thick, white cloud. He tried to hold tightly to the wheel even as he automatically kept his foot on the brake, but there was nothing he could do—

The truck flipped again and again, and it flew through the air as it rolled. Over and over.

And Jamie wasn't screaming any longer. She wasn't making a single sound.

There was only—

Impact. The truck slammed into the trees on the side of the road. More glass shattered. More air bags flew out.

Then there was just silence.

HIS HEART WAS racing in his chest, so fast, so hard. He jumped from his car and rushed toward the wrecked truck. It was smashed and on its side. He'd deliberately targeted the driver. The man was the one he'd wanted to take out, and he had to make sure that Jamie was all right.

She's fine. I didn't hit her side of the vehicle. Jamie is just fine.

It was just that…he hadn't anticipated the truck would flip over. He hadn't thought about that. And there was so much silence now. His booted feet stepped on broken glass. On shards of metal. As he approached the truck, he pulled down his ski mask, just in case. In case anyone drove by, in case the man was still alive, in case...

I don't see Jamie.

He crept closer to the truck. He could see the male. It looked as if the guy had been knocked out. Blood dripped over his closed eyes. The air bags had deflated. As he stretched his hand through the broken windshield, he shoved those bags out of his way. *Jamie, Jamie...*

He heard the roar of an engine in the distance. Another car, dammit. Coming this way.

But he'd just seen Jamie's face. Her eyes were closed, too. He stretched out his gloved hand, reaching out to her. He couldn't tell if she was breathing. She had to be breathing. His Jamie. She had to be okay. He hadn't meant for her to get hurt. It was all that jerk's fault—the man driving. He should have been more careful. He should have stopped the roll of the truck. He should have—

His fingers slid over her neck. The damn glove was in the way. He needed to feel her silken skin beneath his fingertips. He was stretching now, extending his body as far as he could, and he could almost feel her pulse, even through the fabric of the glove. Jamie, alive, his to touch and—

"Get the hell away from her!"

The truck's driver wasn't unconscious, not anymore. He was surging up, trying to heave the crushed metal out of his way.

And Jamie was stirring, too, moaning softly as her lashes fluttered.

I'll see you soon, Jamie. Soon.

"WHAT...HAPPENED?" Jamie muttered as her eyes opened. "I—" A man with a ski mask had his hand stretched out toward her. Jamie screamed and struck out at him. He leaped back, rushing away, and she twisted and shoved against the prison that surrounded her. Frantic now, she fought and fought and—

"Jamie, Jamie, it's okay!"

She froze. The mad drumming of her heartbeat filled her ears.

"He's gone," Davis said, his voice strong. Flat. "He just drove away, though I doubt he'll get far. He hit us damn hard, and the front of his ride has to be wrecked."

She was shaking.

"I lost my phone, and I'm...pinned. But I'll get out," Davis said, his words coming faster now. "Just give me—" she heard the grind of metal "—a minute..."

That metal kept grinding. Kept screeching and then—

Davis was gone.

"Davis?" She turned, searching for him. The deflated air bags sagged around her. She pushed, trying to get them out of her way. Her legs were trapped by the dash, and she was frantically trying to slide out. *"Davis!"* He didn't answer. Had he gone after the guy in the ski mask? *No, Davis, don't leave me.* Not while she was trapped. Helpless.

He'd been reaching for me. If I hadn't woken up, would he have killed me?

Nausea was rolling in her stomach. Twisting. Shaking.

"Are you hurt?"

She let out a little scream. Then, "Don't do that!" Jamie snapped at Davis. He'd gone around the wrecked truck. Stopped on her side. Scared the ever-living hell out of her. "Don't disappear on me!"

He yanked open her door. It nearly fell right off, but Jamie still couldn't get out. The dash had sunk in around her legs.

"Are you hurt?" Davis said again.

She looked up at him. "You're bleeding." A gash over his eye.

"It's nothing. You, Jamie. You…" He pushed against the dash. "Sweetheart, are you hurt?"

She liked it when he called her sweetheart. His voice deepened, and just the faintest hint of warm emotion slid through the word.

When he used that endearment, it sounded as if he cared. She needed someone to care right then. "Not hurt," she whispered. "Just scared. He was right in front of me." A ski mask had covered his face. His hand had been so close to her. *Had he touched me?* She couldn't remember.

Jamie shoved against the dash now, too, desperate to get out. "He could come back." Any minute. "I have to get out! I have to get out!" Because she didn't want to be trapped when he came back for her, or, even worse, what if he came back and tried to hurt Davis again? He'd hit them on Davis's side. A brutal attack that she hadn't expected.

But I should have. Henry doesn't care who gets in his way. He won't stop until he has exactly what he wants.

And she knew he wanted her to suffer.

The dash groaned, and her legs slipped free. She would have fallen from the truck if Davis hadn't been there. He scooped her into his arms. Held her tight. Then he was running. Carrying her even as she tried to slide free and walk on her own.

"We need to get clear...I can smell gas."

And so could she. She stopped fighting him, and Davis rushed them to the other side of the road, which was littered with glass and metal. So much debris. And when she looked over his shoulder at the wreckage, she couldn't believe they'd both gotten out of that mess alive. Too close. *Too close.*

She heard the rumble of an engine approaching them.

Her hold tightened on Davis. "What if it's him?" Jamie whispered. "What if he's coming back?"

Davis slid her down to the ground. He pushed her behind his body.

He needed to forget that whole human shield bit. They needed a weapon. They needed—

Brakes squealed. Jamie shot onto her toes and peered over Davis's shoulder.

"What happened?" Stephanie jumped from the SUV. "Are you hurt?" Then she was running toward them.

Jamie's shoulders slumped as relief swept through her. It wasn't the man in the mask. It was Stephanie, and Davis had already taken the woman's phone and he was calling 911. She could hear him relaying what happened to the operator.

Stephanie touched Jamie's shoulder. "What can I do?"

"I'm fine." Just scratches. Bruises. A few

sore spots for tomorrow. She and Davis were both alive, and that was what mattered.

Henry did this. Henry's come after me... because he told me that he'd never let me go. Now she understood, though, that he wasn't just after her because in his twisted mind, they belonged together. He was hunting her down because he wanted to kill her.

"THE COPS FOUND the abandoned car on Gunter Road," Sullivan said as he stared over at Davis with an unreadable gaze. "I'm thinking he had another ride waiting there, or maybe he even had a partner who drove him away. The cops are searching the vehicle for fingerprints now, and we'll see what they turn up."

The nurse finished stitching Davis's arm. "There. All done." She gave him a faint smile.

"What about Jamie?" he immediately asked. He'd wanted to stay with her, but they'd been separated at the hospital. Once the cops had been called in, all hell had truly broken loose on the old road. Uniforms had swarmed, ambulances had flocked to the scene, and he'd fought to stay close to Jamie.

"She's being examined," the nurse assured him. She was young, probably in her early twenties, with dark hair that fell in a bob to her chin. "You can stay in the waiting room until she's done."

He wanted to stay *with* Jamie. But after the nurse bustled out, he zeroed in his gaze on his brother. Now that they were alone, he could lay all his cards on the table. "I was dazed, just for a few moments." He'd shaken off that dizziness after the truck stopped rolling and then... "He was right there. Reaching for her. Jamie's eyes were closed, and I was trapped. I was afraid..." He clenched his hand and felt the faint pull of the new stitches. "I was afraid he'd kill her right in front of me."

A muscle flexed along Sullivan's jaw. "This isn't some robber. I think we can just ditch that whole theory."

Yes, they could. Her home had been burned not as some part of a robbery strategy. And they'd been attacked...no accidental hit. "She's being hunted."

Sullivan started to speak, then shook his head.

"What?" Davis marched closer to him. "Say it."

"He aimed for your side, bro. Not hers. If someone's being hunted, I think that person might just be you." His eyes glinted. "We need to examine this situation more. Because when I get a phone call telling me that my brother was nearly killed…"

"I'm fine."

"Because you got lucky! He wasn't playing, man. I saw the scene. He wanted to take out you. And if he'd succeeded, what do you think would have happened to your precious Jamie then?" He yanked a hand through his hair. "No, we need to look at this whole case again. Every single bit of it. Call in the whole family. Because there's more here than meets the eye."

"Sully—"

"I think she's lying to you."

Davis stilled. "No."

"I started digging into Henry Westport's life… From all accounts, the guy is still up in Connecticut. For the past few years, he's been a model damn citizen. He's set up dozens of charities, he helps people who are struggling and—"

"Surfaces can lie." Jamie had told him that, but Davis already knew that truth. So did Sullivan. "People show the world only what they want to be seen. The dark spots on a person's soul…they stay hidden."

Sullivan nodded. "Exactly. They do. And I know it can be tempting to fall for a pair of big blue eyes, but, man, we need to learn all the facts of this case. Before you get in too deep, I have to be sure that we can trust this woman. The last thing I want is for you to get caught up in—"

"Someone is after her! Whether it's Westport or some other jerk, Jamie is in danger. She needs our help." That was all there was to it. "Now, I'm going to find her. And I'd appreciate it if you didn't glare suspiciously at her every moment." Because he knew his brother. "I trust her. Isn't that enough?"

He strode past Sullivan, but he caught his brother's growled words. "No, it's not," Sullivan said.

Davis swung back toward him.

"Not when your life is threatened. Not when you're bringing this woman to our ranch. Hasn't our family seen enough heartache? I don't trust her, plain and simple. I don't think she should be brought right into the fold. The more I dig, the more the stories seem to twist about her. I don't—"

Davis heard the rustle of footsteps just beyond the door. *No, no—*

He rushed for the door. Yanked it open. The footsteps weren't just rustling then. They were running. *Jamie* was running down that tiled hospital corridor. She was nearly at the elevator.

"Maybe you should let her go," Sullivan muttered.

The hell he would. "And maybe you should stop letting that darkness eat you alive. Because you didn't use to be such a cold SOB." Harsh words for his brother but...

Sullivan had gone too far. He'd hurt Jamie. Davis rushed after her. "Jamie, stop!"

She stepped into the elevator. Whirled to face him. Hell, the way he was barreling down that corridor, he expected security to tackle him at any moment.

Jamie reached out, and he saw her press the control panel inside the elevator. The doors started to close.

No. He surged forward and threw out his hand. His fingers slipped through the closing doors, setting off the sensors. The doors slid right back open.

Jamie retreated a step. Her eyes had never seemed bigger, and she looked...hurt. Scared.

Of me?

"You know I won't hurt you." He stepped into the elevator. Davis looked over his shoulder. Sullivan stood in the hallway, watching them. He tossed a glare back at his brother, then Davis leaned forward and pressed that control panel, sealing them inside the elevator. "And, for the record, Sullivan doesn't know what the hell he's talking about, okay? Just forget him."

"He knows more than you think." Jamie's voice was whisper soft. "I'm so sorry, Davis. You were hurt because of me. You could have died because I tried to bring you into my nightmare."

Now, that kind of talk just wasn't going to fly with him. "Do you think I'm worried about a little danger?" And he eased closer to her. So close that their bodies brushed. So close that he could feel her warmth sliding over him. "If so, then guess again." He was too well acquainted with danger to ever fear it.

Her breath caught. "There's more about me...that you don't know."

"Then, tell me all your secrets, Jamie. Tell me every single one."

She shook her head. The doors opened behind him. Davis didn't move.

"I've already told you too much," she said, her voice husky as it seemed to slide right over him. "And I dragged you into this mess, just like I did before...with him."

Him?

"It ends. I'm ending it." Her chin lifted. "I

don't want to hire you any longer. We're... we're done. Send me a bill for what I owe you." She rushed past him.

A bill? Seriously? He turned slowly and followed her out. They were on the main lobby level, and she was hurrying toward the sliding glass doors that would lead her to the street. "You think a bill will cover things?"

She stopped, shook her head, then glanced back at him. "How can it? You nearly died... and your truck..." Her shoulders straightened. "I'll pay for it, I promise. I have money saved. I'll—I'll cover that and anything else I owe you."

Now she was making him angry. He had to unclench his back teeth as he closed in on her. A security guard stood near the main entrance to the hospital, and he was already casting suspicious glances toward Davis.

"He's going to come after you again," Davis said, his voice low, carrying only to Jamie's ears. "What are you going to do then? Aren't you tired of running?"

"Yes." She turned toward him. "But I'm also tired of seeing people I care about get hurt. I should have thought about the cost to you. I didn't. I just pulled you right into the cross fire, and I'm sorry."

"I can handle the cross fire." Without a

damn doubt. He'd been through more than his share of hell, both in his time as a SEAL and after he'd started up McGuire Securities with his family. "You don't need to worry about me."

"But that's just it," Jamie said, and her smile was sad. "I do worry about you. I think that I could come to care for you a great deal, Davis. And I just can't let that happen."

What. The. Hell?

"So, goodbye." She surprised him then. As she kept doing. Jamie put her hands on his shoulders. She leaned up on her toes, and she kissed him. Not a deep, passionate kiss. Tender and soft. Gentle.

Wistful.

A might-have-been kiss.

"Take care, Davis. Watch out for your family and watch out for yourself." Her blue gaze was shaded in secrets and mysteries. "And don't worry about me. I'm a survivor." Then she backed away.

"Jamie!"

She hurried toward the security guard. Then she was gone.

He stared after her. No, no way. She hadn't just…left him.

His steps felt wooden as he followed her.

He watched as Jamie jumped into the back of a cab. The cab rushed away.

She thought it would be that easy? Knowing that she was in danger, the woman seriously thought he'd just let her vanish? That was insulting.

He lifted his hand. Hailed the next cab. When he slid into the backseat, he said, "Follow the cab in front of us. Don't even think of losing that woman."

Because he wasn't the type of man who was going to let a little danger scare him away. He also wasn't about to let Jamie face that hunter on her own. He didn't like the shadows in Jamie's eyes. Those echoes of pain didn't belong in her blue gaze. He'd find the man who was terrorizing her, he'd uncover all of Jamie's secrets—good and bad, and he *would* keep her safe.

His taxi surged away from the curb.

DAVIS WAS BLIND.

Sullivan watched as his brother gave chase. He'd taken the second elevator downstairs, and he'd been lingering close by in the lobby. He'd heard the faint goodbye talk that Jamie had given his brother. Davis should have let the woman walk away—let her and her danger go.

But he hadn't.

Despite his tough exterior, Davis had a weakness, one that Sullivan knew well. Davis was out to save the world...or at least, the world's victims. He could never turn away from someone in need. And when a woman like Jamie appeared, Sullivan knew Davis's protective instincts would have gone into overdrive.

But Sullivan understood how deceptive a fragile appearance could be. He knew that those who looked weak...well, they were actually the most vicious ones out there. Davis was getting tangled up in Jamie, and while Sullivan had initially liked the pretty vet, now his suspicions were on full alert.

Family came first for Sullivan. Always had, always would. And he wasn't about to stand back while his brother was in danger.

Since he was the youngest brother, most folks probably thought the others looked after him. They were wrong. He'd spent years protecting his brothers. Keeping their secrets. Even keeping some secrets *from* them. And he'd continue his silent vigil. Someone had to keep the family together. Someone had to keep them all safe.

Someone had to protect them from the dangers they never saw coming.

Chapter Five

"You could have saved a ton of cab fare," Davis drawled when Jamie stepped out of her taxi. She spun around and saw him just a few feet behind her. She wasn't particularly surprised. After all, she'd noticed the other cab tailing her as she took the long, winding drive that led to the McGuire ranch.

"We could've driven out here together," Davis continued.

Jamie motioned toward the gate. "Will you just type in the code to let me inside? I need to get my dog. And my car." Then she'd be driving right out of his life.

He strode toward her. She tensed, but he didn't try to touch her. Instead, he leaned forward, reached around her and typed in the code. "Let's just take one cab up to the house," he murmured. "Makes more sense."

"Fine." She didn't particularly care about making sense. She just needed to get Jinx and get her car. Then she'd start figuring out her next move. Before she could pay her driver, Davis beat her to the punch. He tossed the guy his cash and waved him away. Her eyes narrowed, but she didn't argue, not then. She climbed into the other cab and didn't say a word, not until they'd been dropped off at the main house and that cab was on its way out.

"Brodie's inside the house," Davis said. "He'll be monitoring security, and he'll make sure the cab gets out of the gate. He would have let you in, too. Next time, just press the buzzer."

There wasn't going to be a next time. "I'll get out of your way immediately," Jamie said. "You don't need to worry." She marched toward the guesthouse—and her dog.

"Oh, but I am worried." He reached out and caught her arm. "I'm worried about you. Someone just tried to kill you, in case you missed that."

It was rather hard to miss the spinning truck and the broken glass. "No." Her lashes lifted, and she stared up into his eyes. "That's where you're wrong. He was trying to kill *you*, not me. You were the target. Just because you were with me. I did that to you. I brought you into his sights even knowing how dangerous that is. *I* did it. And I am sorrier than I can ever say." She kept hearing that terrible screech of metal. Kept feeling that bone-jarring impact. She'd screamed and reached out for Davis, but it had been too late. Tears stung her eyes at the memory. "Just let me go, okay?" She pulled away from him.

But he just reached out to her again. This time, both of his hands wrapped around her shoulders. "What if I don't want to?"

"What?"

"What if I don't want to watch you walk away? What if I'm tired of holding back, and I want to reach out and take the thing I've been wanting for so long?"

She was still nervous about his intentions—his feelings. He'd barely spoken to her over the past year. Sure, they'd encountered each other plenty of times, but he'd usually just nodded or murmured some kind of curt greeting or—

"I don't know what to say to you," Davis confessed, and his voice was that rough rumble she found so sexy. "Because I'm too afraid of scaring you away."

Davis didn't scare her. The thought of something happening to him...*that* terrified her.

"You think I didn't already realize you

were running from someone? Even before Ava's wedding night?" His hold tightened on her. "I could see it in your eyes. Anytime people got too close to you, a haunted, wary look slid into your gaze."

But she'd tried to be so careful.

"I heard about the guys who asked you out."

"What?" How had he even—

"Grant's wife, Scarlett, knows your assistant." He gave a little wince. "So maybe I asked. Maybe I needed to know if I'd already missed my shot with you."

"You wanted a shot with me?" All of this was news to her. "Since when?"

"Since the first moment I saw you. You were out here at the ranch, taking care of Lady, and I walked up. You looked back at me, and, hell, for a minute, I forgot every damn word in my head."

Impossible. Not confident, in-control Davis. He'd barely noticed her. She remembered that first day. It had been the first time she realized Davis and Brodie were twins. Identical twins. Only...

I didn't want Brodie when I met him. I looked at Davis...and saw everything that I'd been missing. Heat. Passion. A desire to melt the cold that had consumed her for so long.

But he'd turned away. Barely spoken to her the rest of the afternoon.

She'd heard gossip about him after that. Or maybe she'd gone looking for gossip. And, oddly enough, she'd gotten it from the same source that he'd used—her assistant, Sylvia Jones. Sylvia had seemed to be an expert on all things McGuire.

"Some folks say he's a killer...you know, because of all that top-secret SEAL work he did." Sylvia had shrugged. *"He's the quiet, intense type, know what I mean?"*

Not really, Jamie hadn't. She'd stayed far away from all the types for too long.

"He's got that laser focus, though." Sylvia had laughed. *"Wonder what it would be like to have that focus locked on you?"*

That focus was currently locked on Jamie. She could see it in his eyes, in the widening of his pupils. Feel it in his touch.

"You'd already been hurt by someone, I knew it. You had the same shadows in your eyes that Ava had."

She wanted to look away from him, to hide those shadows, but she couldn't.

"So I was trying to bide my time. Wait for the right moment. At the wedding, I thought, maybe it was time then. You danced with me. You kissed me."

She hadn't danced with a man like that in longer than she wanted to remember. She hadn't lowered her guard. Lowering that guard was too dangerous.

"And then your past came back. That past is trying to take you away from me now." His head leaned toward her. "Don't let it, Jamie. Don't."

"Davis—"

She heard a door slam. Then the thud of footsteps.

Davis swore. "My brother has the worst timing in the world." But he didn't let her go. He didn't turn to look toward the thud of those steps.

"Sullivan called me," Brodie announced as he drew closer. "Dammit, are you both all right?"

"Fine," Davis said, still staring down at Jamie. "Nothing a few stitches couldn't fix."

"This time," Jamie whispered, her heart aching. "But what about next time?" She shook her head. "I'm sorry, Davis, but I have to go." Then she pulled from him. She kept her head up as she hurried toward the guest-house and her waiting dog.

She didn't look back. She'd learned never

to do that. But she was so tempted, so very tempted, to look back at Davis just one more time.

"JEEZ, BRODIE!" Jennifer McGuire hurried down the steps. "Didn't I tell you to give them a few minutes? Now look what you've done." She gestured toward Jamie's fleeing back. "The woman is running when they were just about to make out!"

If only. Davis stared after Jamie. She wasn't relenting. She was bound and determined to leave him. And with that creep on her trail, the last thing she needed was to be on her own.

"I was worried about him," Brodie muttered. "From what Sullivan said, he was nearly killed." He marched closer to Davis. "And when something like that happens…" His hand curled around Davis's shoulder, and Davis swung around to face his brother. "You call me." Worry shone in Brodie's eyes. Eyes exactly like Davis's own. "You let me know right away what's happening with you."

"I'm all right," he said softly. "You know it takes more than a few scratches to slow me down."

"And more than a totaled truck?" Brodie asked as his lips tightened. "Because Grant went to the scene. He took pictures and texted them to me."

Figured. When one McGuire was hurt, they all swarmed, especially their eldest brother, Grant. After their parents' death, Grant had taken it upon himself to keep the family together.

"You're not just going to let the woman walk away, are you?" Jennifer asked as she pressed closer. Jennifer had been an enigma when she first turned up at McGuire Securities. On the surface, she'd appeared to be a pampered socialite. It wasn't until much later that they'd all learned the truth. Jennifer had been a secret agent, living a carefully constructed cover life. When she'd been undercover, Brodie had saved her. So when danger stalked her again, she'd turned to him once more.

And the two had fallen in love.

Now Jennifer worked with them at McGuire Securities. When it came to ferreting out information, the woman was in a class by herself. He knew that both she and Sullivan had already been digging into Jamie's past. He just hoped their inquiries hadn't attracted the wrong kind of attention.

"Davis!" Jennifer shook her head. "The woman is getting her dog, and she's about to drive off into who knows what kind of trouble! A fire, a hit-and-run… What's going to be next? And will she just walk away from another attack? Or will the next one take her out?"

"I can't force her to stay with me," he gritted out. "Hell, I think the woman just fired me." He'd never been fired before. Davis didn't particularly like the feeling.

"What?" Jennifer's mouth formed an O of surprise. Her deep brown eyes showed her shock. Then her lips twitched. "Okay, if she weren't in danger, I'd say that was seriously awesome. Someone firing a McGuire brother…priceless."

Both Brodie and Davis turned to frown at her.

She just smiled. Her dark hair was pulled back at the nape of her neck, and her golden skin gleamed in the setting sun. "What? You guys really can get too cocky, you know. Sometimes you need a dose of reality to knock you back down to earth."

He wasn't cocky. When it came to Jamie, he was…nervous. "I want her safe. She'll have no protection when she leaves. She—"

Jennifer caught his arm. She *pushed* him. For someone so small, she really packed a lot of strength in her little body. "So stop her.

Stop being all stoic, and just ask the woman to stay with you. Don't even make it about the guy terrorizing her. Make it about you. About Jamie. Ask her for one night." She nodded. "I'd lay odds that she won't deny you that. I have it on pretty big authority that when the McGuires want something, they can be quite charming."

But he didn't want to charm Jamie. Didn't want to lie to her. Didn't—

"She's getting into her car."

Hell. He took off running. As he drew closer to her vehicle, Davis could hear Jinx's excited barks. She'd already put the dog in the backseat and was about to slide in behind the steering wheel.

He reached out and caught her hand.

Jamie stilled.

"One night." That was what Jennifer said he should ask for, so he'd start with that. Sure, he wanted more—so much more—but he'd take it one step at a time. "You're not endangering anyone by staying out here for one more night. The sun is already starting to set. You're safe here. I'm safe."

Her eyelashes—the woman had incredibly long lashes—slowly lifted.

"One night," he said again. "What's it going

to hurt? Nothing. You can rest here. Stay at the guesthouse. No one will bother you."

She seemed to be relenting. He could see it in her gaze.

So back off and let her think.

"You can always fire me tomorrow," he told her.

She bit her lip. Damn. He'd like to soothe that little pain away. There was so much he wanted to do with her but...

First, I just want to keep her safe. I want to take some of that pain from her eyes.

She was silent. Jinx whined a bit in the backseat.

"You don't even know that you'd find a hotel room tonight," he pushed. "We have room here. And no one will get past our security." *Stay. Stay with me.*

Then, after a long, tense moment, she nodded.

His breath left his lungs in a relieved rush. Well, hot damn. Jennifer truly should be a gambler.

JAMIE HADN'T RETURNED to her clinic. She'd gone...presumably with the man. He knew the man's identity now. He'd done his research. He'd lingered. Learned from a chatty cop that the man's name was Davis McGuire.

Apparently, Davis McGuire owned some kind of PI firm in Austin. So maybe the guy wasn't involved with Jamie. Maybe he was just the hired help. That made more sense.

But I'm still angry with you, sweet Jamie. Because she'd lied to him for so long. Lied about him. She would suffer for that.

But only at first.

He already had started the process of digging into Davis McGuire's past. Early on, he'd learned that no one was perfect. He wasn't the only one with demons. Everyone had them. Some demons were just stronger than others.

How strong would Davis's demons turn out to be? He couldn't wait to find out.

Some demons…they could drive a man right to the very edge of reason…and then over the cliff into madness.

NIGHT HAD FALLEN. Again. A night filled with a million stars. Jamie stood on the porch of the guesthouse, and she stared up at those stars. When she'd been a kid, she loved wishing on stars. Closing her eyes and hoping. For so long, she'd believed those wishes would come true.

Then she'd learned the truth.

There were some things that even wishes couldn't change.

So she'd stopped staring up at the stars and making those impossible dreams.

But for this night, she was tempted...so very tempted...to try again. To make just one more wish.

Jamie stared at the stars. *I wish...*

She heard the snap of a twig. Her body iced, and she whirled around.

"Sorry," Davis said. The lights from the guesthouse spilled onto him. "I didn't mean to scare you. I just wanted to check on you before I turned in for the night."

Her heart raced in her chest.

"Do you need anything?"

Yes, actually, but was she really supposed to say...*you*? A woman with far more experience would do that. A woman with casual confidence. But Jamie wasn't that woman. Jamie hadn't even been with a lover in years.

Her last two experiences had ended horribly. Tragically.

She'd been too afraid to get close to anyone else.

But...

I want to be close to him. And he was right there. Close enough to touch. Close enough to kiss.

"All right," Davis drawled. "Well, if you need me during the night, just remember that I'm nearby." He turned away. "I'll come if you call."

Stop being afraid! She'd agreed to one night, and…why not have everything she wanted on this last one night? "I need you."

He stopped. Didn't look back at her. "I don't think I heard you right."

"I think you did." Her cheeks were flaming, and her knees were knocking together, but she'd started this, so she'd have to see where it led. He'd been clear that he desired her before. That kiss they'd shared—right down there near the lake—had rocked her whole system. Why not have this time together?

One night.

He'd convinced her to stay. Now she had to convince him that they should spend these hours together.

One night.

Then they could both move on—no regrets, no looking back. Just good memories. She could sure use some of those.

Slowly, Davis turned to face her. Half of his face was in shadows now, and that darkness just gave him a dangerous edge. A sexy edge.

"What is it that you need, Jamie?" His

voice had deepened. He strode toward her. Slowly, like a predator, closing in on his prey.

She held her ground. Locked her knees. Waited until he was right in front of her. Then Jamie grabbed her courage with both hands. For an instant, she'd pretend to be that confident, assured woman. "You. I want you, Davis." As she'd never really wanted anyone else. She'd never touched someone and seemed to ignite, the way she did with him. "Stay with me tonight?"

"Jamie." Her name was a growl. So low and deep. The rough sound sent a shiver down her spine. That shiver wasn't caused by fear, not at all, but by a primal awareness within her. He wanted her.

She could see that need blazing in his eyes. Feel it in the tension around them.

But he wasn't touching her. She wanted him to kiss her. To lock his arms around her and pull her close. She needed that.

He wasn't moving.

"Don't you want to be with me?" Jamie asked. There wasn't room for pride or games. She didn't know how to play those games, anyway. She only knew how to tell him the truth about her feelings.

"More than you can know," Davis said. The sound of his voice was melting her. A rough, rasping voice. One that she could so easily imagine coming from the darkness of a bedroom.

She smiled at him. And, because he wasn't making the next move, she did. Jamie stepped toward him. Her hand pressed to his chest.

"This isn't a game." He'd stiffened beneath her touch. "Be very sure you understand what I want."

If her heart beat much faster, her whole body would shake. "Why don't you tell me what you want?" she asked.

"I want you, wild and reckless for me. Open completely. Giving me everything that you have."

And her body *was* shaking.

"I want to take you so completely that we both lose ourselves. But I'm not easy, Jamie. I'm not the kind of guy who goes for soft whispers in the dark."

No, she hadn't thought that he would be. "What kind of guy are you?"

"The kind who'll make you scream. The kind who will give you so much pleasure you don't think you can stand it." He eased closer to her. And, finally, he touched her. His callused fingertips slid down her cheek, then down her neck. His fingers brushed over her frantically racing pulse. "And when you're sure that you can't take any more, that's when I'll push you right over the edge."

That sounded pretty fabulous to her. "Then what are you waiting for?"

She saw it—saw his control crack. He lunged toward her, wrapped her in his arms and kissed her. Not sweet and easy, just as he'd said. But hard and deep and with enough passion to make her toes curl. It was exactly the kind of kiss she'd wanted from him.

And it was just the start.

They stumbled into the guesthouse. He shut the door. Punched in a security code for her. Then he pushed her up against the nearest wall. He kept kissing her. His hands caught hers. He pinned her wrists to the wall, and his mouth seduced her. No other word for it—his lips, his tongue...*seduction*. She arched toward him even as a moan built in her throat. She was wearing a pair of jeans, so was he, but she could feel the hot length of his arousal pressing against her.

He wanted her, just as fiercely as she wanted him.

But then he pulled back.

"Davis—"

He caught the hem of her shirt. Lifted it over her head and tossed it toward the sofa. She

wore a light blue bra and when his gaze slid to
the curve of her breasts, Jamie's breath caught.

She had scars. One scar across the top of
her left breast. One on her rib cage. Two on
her stomach. One on each side of her body.
Lines that reminded her of the past. Lines that
she hated for him to see.

But Davis had stepped back. That hot green
stare swept over her. "Beautiful," he said, his
voice guttural, and she felt beautiful in that
moment. Her fears vanished because he was
staring at her with a ferocious desire, as if
he'd never seen anyone else who tempted him
so much. And she knew it wasn't true, but she
still glowed beneath his stare.

He unhooked her bra. Threw it toward
her discarded shirt. Then he bent his head
and kissed her breast. She sucked in a sharp
breath as pleasure seemed to whip right
through her body. Her nipples were tight, aching, and when he touched her, with his fingers, with his lips, with his tongue, he pushed
her desire even higher.

Her hips rocked against him. She wanted
the jeans gone. Hers. His. She wanted nothing
between them. Jamie wanted to feel the hot,
hard length of him against her. In her. Her
hands jerked down and her fingers pushed

between their bodies. She unhooked the snap of his jeans, pulled down the zipper—

"Not so fast..."

No, she wanted fast. She wanted him right then and there. Against the wall. On the couch. On the floor. It didn't matter to her. She just wanted him.

"I thought about you for so long," Davis said. "I want to see you, all of you."

She wanted to see him, too. That was why she was trying to get his clothes off. She wanted to see him and touch him and—

He was carrying her. Davis lifted her up as if she weighed nothing, a huge turn-on, but she already felt as if she was on fire for him. He carried her to the bedroom. Lowered her until her feet touched the floor. Then he backed away and began to strip.

He grabbed his shirt. Lifted it up. But paused. "I've got scars, too," he said, that deep voice of his rumbling. "Just be warned..."

Like she cared about his scars. Like she—

He dropped the shirt.

She wondered if her jaw dropped, too. Because Davis was seriously built. Wide shoulders. Abs of steel. Not a six-pack. A twelve-pack? Just how often did the guy work out?

"Do they bother you?"

Wait, what? Then she realized he meant the scars. And she could see the white lines. Some looked as if they'd been from…from knife attacks. She knew because they were similar to her own marks. Others were bigger—maybe from gunshots? "They don't bother me," she whispered as she touched him. Her fingers slid over his abs. *Made of hot steel.* She lightly caressed one of his scars. "I just hate you suffered any pain."

"I'm not suffering now." And his head bent. He pressed a kiss to her neck. A white-hot touch that had her toes curling.

She reached for the snap of his jeans again, but he beat her. He shoved the jeans down. Kicked out of his shoes and was standing there, naked, as he pressed a kiss to the curve of her neck.

And then he took care of her clothes. Carefully, sensually, he pushed down her jeans. She'd kicked away her shoes while he was carrying her to the bedroom. Her jeans fell in a puddle on the floor, and she stood there, clad in her panties before him.

"You are so beautiful."

The back of her legs brushed against the mattress. His fingers curled around her hips even as his eyes blazed down on her.

He kissed her again, a hot, deep, open-mouthed kiss that had her holding tightly to his shoulders. They tumbled onto the bed together, and the mattress dipped beneath them. His legs slid between hers, and Davis kissed a scorching path down her throat. She arched toward him, her whole body taut and ready. "Now, Davis, now!"

"Not yet." He stroked her. Kissed her. He'd said it would be rough and wild, and it was. Her hands flew back and grasped the bedspread. She fisted that material in her grip, straining because she felt so out of control. The way he was touching her, kissing her, *all* of her...she wasn't going to be able to take much more.

Then he slid away.

"No!"

But she heaved up and saw that he'd grabbed protection from his jeans. He tore the foil wrapper, then came back to her. Her legs wrapped around him. She arched her hips, and when he drove into her, Jamie lost her breath.

Their gazes locked.

She saw his need. The hot passion. The desperate yearning. And she knew he read all of that in her stare, too. He had to feel it. The desire was too much, the need consuming her.

He withdrew, thrust, and the rhythm between them became frantic. Harder. Wilder. Her nails dug into his shoulders as she arched her hips toward him and took him in deep. She wanted everything that he had to give— and she was giving herself to him, completely, freely.

No fear.

No hesitations.

Nothing but pleasure.

The release swept her up, and she called out his name. Her body shook as the climax lashed her. She held on to him, gripping him even more tightly as the rest of the world fell away.

Then he was growling out her name. Driving into her, deeper, kissing her, and she could taste his pleasure.

The drumming of her heartbeat filled Jamie's ears. Slowly, that frenzied pounding faded. Davis braced himself on his arms and stared down at her.

She tried to think of something to say, but Jamie was far too out of control for that. Her body still quivered, and her emotions were all over the place. So she didn't speak. She sank her fingers into the thickness of his hair and pulled him closer. Then she kissed him.

And the desire built once more.

Chapter Six

"I'm sorry," Jamie whispered. "So sorry… it's my fault…"

Davis opened his eyes and saw that streaks of sunlight were falling onto the bed. He turned his head to look at Jamie. She was curled in bed beside him, a sheet pulled up to the curve of her breasts. Her lashes were still closed, but her head moved restlessly against the pillow.

"Sorry," she muttered again. "My fault… I—I told him… *Sorry…*" Her breath heaved out. "Don't, *don't*—Warren, don't!"

Warren?

Then she screamed. A loud, terrified cry.

"Jamie!" He shook her once, lightly. "Sweetheart, wake up. It's just a nightmare."

Her breath heaved out, and her eyes flew open. At first she stared at him in horror, not even a hint of recognition on her face. But then she blinked, and some of that terror faded from her gaze. "I'm sorry," she whispered, voice husky. "I—I should have warned you about those."

The sheet had fallen, revealing what he truly thought were absolutely perfect breasts, but Jamie pulled away from him before he could admire them longer. She twisted and rose from the bed, taking the sheet with her. He watched, silent, as she secured that sheet, toga-style, around her.

"I don't ever really have sweet dreams." She bit her lower lip, a lip that still appeared a bit swollen from the night before. He'd been frantic for her mouth, for her. He'd kissed her again and again, just as he'd gotten lost in her body again and again. "I should have told you to leave sooner, so you didn't have to deal with…this."

His brows rose, and Davis made no move to exit the bed. "A nightmare? It's not a big deal. Everyone has them." He had his share. But, curious now, he asked, "Is that what you do, though? You don't let your lovers stay the night?" And even as he asked the question, a hard tightness pushed down onto his chest. He didn't want to know about her other lovers. The men who'd been lucky enough to see the pleasure flash on her face and to watch her go wild as she—

"Lovers?" Jamie shook her head. "I, um, I probably should have told you. I'm not exactly very experienced at this sort of thing."

He blinked. She'd driven him insane the night before. Given him the best releases he'd ever had.

"After Henry, I was with…I was with one other man. Back in college. We were together for a few months but that just—" She broke off and looked away. "It didn't work out. I didn't get close to anyone after that. It just seemed safer that way."

Safer. Now, that was a damn odd way of putting things.

"I guess with you…" Jamie lowered her gaze to the bed. The bed they'd wrecked. "I wanted to take a risk. I wanted you more than I wanted safety."

He rose from the bed. Naked, he stalked to her. "You know you can have both." She needed to see that. "You can have me, and—" his fingers trailed over her bare shoulder "—I'll always keep you safe."

Her lips parted.

"I don't want last night to be a one-time deal." No, he was already desperate to have her again and again. "I don't want you running from your past any longer. You have a life here. A home. A practice." *You have me.* "We can find this guy, Jamie. We can stop him."

"What if someone gets hurt? Because of me? Because I—"

"It's not because of you." The guilt in her voice pierced him to the core. "You didn't do this, Jamie. It was some sick freak who got obsessed with you. You were just a kid. You didn't—"

"That's not what they said," she whispered.

He frowned at her. "What?"

"Do you think you know me?" Jamie's head tilted to the side as she stared up at him.

"Yes." He did. "I know you're smart and dedicated. I know you care about the people here, that you—"

"Everyone has a dark side, hidden beneath the surface. Even me."

He could see the faint mark he'd left on her neck. He knew there was plenty of passion to Jamie, but a darkness? No, he didn't see it.

"I almost killed Henry."

He shook his head. Sullivan had been digging, but he hadn't found anything to suggest that Jamie had gone after the other man.

"After he shot my brother, I took the gun from him. Henry was just standing there, staring at me, and smiling. *Smiling* while my brother bled out. He told me… 'I found you, just like you wanted.' As if I'd wanted him to hunt me down."

"Jamie—"

"I had the gun in my hand, and I think I would have shot him. My fingers were tightening around the trigger. Then campus security rushed up. They surrounded us. They took us both away." She looked down at her hands. Stared at them for a moment as if they weren't even her own. "You're not supposed to want to kill someone, but I did. If those security men hadn't arrived, I would have shot him. I would have—"

He caught her hands in his. "He was terrorizing you. Your reaction was normal." He knew that better than most. With all of his times in battle, he understood exactly how hard a mind could be pushed—and that push could only go so far until the instinct for survival kicked in and obliterated everything else. "You wanted to live, sweetheart, you wanted—"

"I wanted him to suffer, the way he'd made me suffer. I wanted to hurt him." Her smile was sad. Bitter. "See, I'm not all sunshine and light."

"No one is." He wanted that jerk to suffer, too. "You think I'm going to judge you for that? Hell, no. I've done things, too. Things that I won't ever forget. In battle, it's kill or be killed. I've seen my share of hell, and I've got the nightmares to prove it." If anyone could understand the dreams that haunted her, it was him. "You're strong, sweetheart. You've had to be in order to survive the pain that has plagued you. But you don't have to keep running. We'll face the man coming after you. We *will* stop him." He needed her to believe that.

The struggle was plain to see on her face. "What if he comes after you again?"

Let him. He'd be ready for the joker. "Then that will be his mistake." Because he'd be ready. He'd make sure to stop the guy, once and for all. "I'm not going to let him hurt me, and I'm sure as hell not going to let him hurt you."

Didn't she understand? Didn't she see how much he needed her? Jamie was becoming so important to him. He didn't want to lose her now.

"Stay," he said, his voice too gruff. He should be using pat lines to persuade her. Should be trying to charm her. But that wasn't him. "Stay with me."

She hesitated. Fear flickered in her gaze. That beautiful gaze. But then...

Jamie nodded.

ONCE SHE WAS back in her office, Jamie realized that she was making a mistake. Jamie was sure of it. She should have closed down her clinic, made arrangements for another vet to see her patients, and she should have left town. Then no one else would have been put in harm's way. She could get to work starting over, someplace new.

But…

I don't want to leave Davis.

Something had happened during their night together. Not just pleasure—though, yes, her body still tingled in some pretty awesome places. But so much more. She'd felt close to him, close enough to confide her darkest fears. And he'd just understood. Accepted. No one had ever done that before. No one had just told her that it was okay…that she was normal…

Stay.

When she was with Davis, Jamie actually felt as if she belonged. Her house had gone up in flames, but she still felt as if she was at home there because of Davis.

"So, um, what's with the guy in the lobby?" Sylvia asked as she tucked a strand of her long red hair behind her ear. "Is there a particular reason Mackenzie McGuire is sitting in our reception area?"

Jamie risked a quick glance over the counter. Her gaze collided with Mac's. She didn't know much about that McGuire brother. He wasn't usually at the ranch. Like his brothers, he was tall, with broad shoulders, dark hair and those intense green eyes. "He's, um... watching out for me." Actually, Mac had been given guard duty. She'd told Davis that she didn't need someone with her every minute, but he'd been adamant. While he was searching the area for Henry, he'd wanted her protected.

And that protection had come in the form of Mac.

"Watching out for you?" Sylvia leaned closer. She peered over at Mac, then gave him a friendly little flutter of her fingers. Mac just frowned back at her. "Right. I heard about the fire." She focused on Jamie. Sylvia's fingers squeezed her shoulder. "You know if you need anything, I'm here. You can even stay with me if you want. I mean, you've probably been bunking at a hotel, and that's just not necessary."

Not so much in a hotel.

But in a bed with Davis.

"I'm your friend," Sylvia continued doggedly. "You know you can count on me."

Yes, she did. "Thanks, Sylvia." Sylvia never

pressured Jamie, she just accepted her. Good. Easy. Sylvia had been welcoming from the instant that Jamie had arrived. They'd met at a local store long before Jamie had hired the woman as her assistant. Sylvia didn't have a mean bone in her body. The woman was friendly to everyone she met.

Even to Mac McGuire.

"So…" Sylvia flipped open her planner. "Looks like we've got a lot of house calls today."

And maybe all of those calls would help to keep Jamie's mind off Henry. Because…

I know he's out there. He has to be close. I can practically feel him watching me.

"ACCORDING TO HIS SECRETARY, Henry West-port was at the family estate in Travers, Connecticut, yesterday," Sullivan said as he paced in front of Davis's desk. They were at McGuire Securities headquarters—Davis, Sullivan, Brodie and Jennifer. "She swears that he hasn't left the city in the past month. Apparently, the guy is working on some big charity project for the homeless, and it's taking up all of his time."

"She could be lying," Jennifer said immediately. "It sure wouldn't be the first time an employee lied for her boss."

The door opened, and Grant stepped inside. Davis had already briefed his older brother on the situation. "I called in some favors and checked the flight records," Grant said, shaking his head. "Unless he is seriously under the radar, Henry Westport hasn't left Travers, at least not by plane. Not commercial and not private. According to all my intel, the guy is at work right now, settled in at Westport Industries and *not* setting fires in Texas."

He was just backing up everything Sullivan had said, but Davis wasn't buying that Henry was clean. His instincts were in overdrive, and they were all screaming that Henry Westport was a serious threat to Jamie. "Then he hired someone," Davis said. "The guy has plenty of money." Enough money that his parents had managed to buy his freedom. "So he tracked Jamie down, and he hired someone to come after her."

Brodie was sitting on the couch next to Jennifer. "Definite possibility." He inclined his head. "So in that case, we need to be monitoring the guy's financials. Because if he's put some kind of hit on Jamie, then we can trace the money and see where it leads."

"We need to find this perp, fast." Davis paced toward the window. "But even if Westport took out a hit on her and he has someone else doing his dirty work, the whole mess still traces back to Henry. He's the one who's obsessed. He's the one we have to stop, he's—"

"There are some things you need to know about Henry," Sullivan said. His voice was stilted, and when Davis glanced over at him, Sullivan's face was expressionless. "I spent the night digging up intel on the case against him." His lips thinned. "It's not as black-and-white as you might think."

Davis squared off against his brother. "The man stabbed Jamie six times. He attacked her. I've seen the scars. I—"

"According to testimony from Henry Westport's parents, Jamie enticed their son. She manipulated him for weeks. Played mind games, deliberately sent him into jealous rages—"

"Stop." Davis had clenched his hands into fists. "What the hell, Sully? Blaming the victim? This isn't you. You know better. You—"

"When Jamie's brother was shot, she told the cops on scene, 'It's my fault. I did this.'"

He remembered the tortured words Jamie had whispered in her sleep. "She meant that she'd brought that jerk into her brother's life. Into her life. She was just a kid, man. Seventeen. She didn't—"

"Has she ever mentioned a man named Sean Nyle to you?"

The others just stared at Davis. He shook his head. "No. Is the name supposed to mean something?"

"He was her lover."

After Henry, I was with...I was with one other man. Back in college. We were together for a few months but that just—it didn't work out. I didn't get close to anyone after that. It just seemed safer that way.

"Want to know why Henry Westport is out on the streets now? It's because Jamie's ex-lover... Sean Nyle...testified at one of his hearings. He said Jamie confessed to manipulating Henry, to playing with his emotions. She hated her parents, and she wanted Henry to help her escape from them, from her whole family. Her wounds were just for show. Not deep enough to kill. She had a whole plan in place and—"

"Stop," Davis snarled. "That's *not* Jamie."

Silence. Thick, uncomfortable.

"How do you know?" Sullivan asked him as he approached with slow but determined steps. "I don't get what's going on between you two. One minute, you're strangers, the next...*you're* almost obsessed with her. But that's what Henry and Sean said she did. I read their accounts. They got caught up in her. Lost. Willing to do *anything* for the woman." His gaze searched Davis's. "Does that sound familiar to you?"

He grabbed Sully's shirtfront. "You don't know her!"

"And neither do you! Not really! Dammit, I'm just asking you to slow down. To be careful. Because you could have died when that car hit you, but she would have just walked away with a scratch or two and—"

Brodie pulled them apart, then took up a protective position right next to Davis.

Always has my back.

"You've changed," Brodie said flatly to Sullivan. "I don't know why, but I've seen it, over the past few months. You didn't used to be like this. You wanted to help, just like we did."

"I still do," Sullivan gritted. "But my family is *first*. I want to know exactly what we're getting involved with here! People lie, they make you think—"

"I lied." Jennifer's voice was soft.

Sullivan swung toward her.

"I pretended to be someone I wasn't for so long. So long that I almost forgot myself." Sadness whispered over her face and deepened even more in her voice. "People can lie for all kinds of reasons…to protect themselves, because they're desperate, because they have no choice."

Sullivan yanked a hand through his hair. "I wasn't talking about you, Jennifer. Hell, you know that. You're family——"

"I wasn't."

Brodie hurried toward her. He put his hand on her shoulder and glared at Sullivan.

"I was a stranger to everyone but Brodie. And when I came back into his life, I brought so much danger with me. People were hurt. I thought I'd lose Brodie." Her hand lifted and curled around Brodie's. "But he fought for me, and I fought for him. We made it. If you'd known the truth about my past from the beginning…" She exhaled and her shoulders sagged. "Would you have told him to walk away from me, too?"

"I—"

"I wouldn't have done it," Brodie said immediately. Then he leaned forward and pressed a quick kiss to Jennifer's temple. "Nothing would have made me leave her. Family or no family."

And Davis felt the same way. "I believe what Jamie has told me." He'd looked into her eyes and seen the truth. "You say this Sean Nyle went to the cops and told them Jamie was some femme fatale? Then I say check *his* financials." Because he had his own suspicions. "The Westports got to Jamie's family before. They like throwing their money around. And I'm betting they did the same thing with him. They followed her. They found her, and they used her relationship with Sean against her."

No wonder you don't trust easily, sweetheart. They kept battering you from all sides.

"Better yet," Davis said, nodding, "let's go find the guy. I'd love to have a little sit-down with Sean." His jaw clenched. "And with Henry." No, he'd love to beat the hell out of that guy.

"Someone needs to fly up to Travers," Grant said. He'd been watching them all, his gaze intent. "And find out for certain... is Henry really there or is he still locked on Jamie? Did he slip down here despite what we're hearing? Is he hunting her right now?"

Jennifer shook her head. "If you confront him directly, and he's *not* the one doing this, that could stir him up again. I mean, if he doesn't know where Jamie is, then we have to keep that information secret. He could track us back here and straight to Jamie."

That was the last thing Davis wanted.

"We have to confirm his whereabouts,"

Grant said grimly. "That's our first step. We need eyes on him. We need to see for certain if he's up there or hiding in the shadows down here." He nodded. "I'll fly up there. I'll see him, but he won't see me."

"And I'll track down Sean," Davis said. He tried to keep the rage out of his voice. Two lovers...two men who'd both hurt Jamie. *His* Jamie.

"I already tracked him," Sullivan said, surprising him. "He's in Houston."

Davis swore. "He's that close?" And he was supposed to buy that as coincidence?

"Moved there about six months ago," Sullivan told him. "And started up a veterinary practice."

And Jamie had moved to town a little over a year before.

His eyes narrowed. "I think I need to take a road trip." Because he was going to get the truth out of Sean Nyle, one way or another.

"I APPRECIATE YOUR keeping watch on me," Jamie said softly. She'd just finished up her rounds at Belmont Ridge, a local farm with the sweetest cows she'd ever seen. Now she and Mac were back in the parking lot of her clinic. "I know this probably isn't the most exciting thing for you...but..."

"Why are you scared of me?"

At Mac's question, Jamie's gaze flew up to his face.

"I can tell, you know. This is the first time you've looked me in the eyes since I started guard duty." His hard lips lifted in a faint smile. "Despite what you may have heard about me, I don't bite."

Jamie wasn't so sure of that. Sylvia had told her that Mac was ex-Delta Force, and the so-called "wildest" McGuire brother. When he'd been a teen, Mac had apparently never met a fight he didn't like.

"I just don't want anyone put at risk for me." She rubbed the back of her neck. "I feel bad, having you out here."

"Risk?" Mac repeated, and he laughed. "I live for that."

And she could see the wildness then. In his eyes—eyes that were darker than Davis's.

"Davis wants you safe, and that's why I'm here. Nothing is going to happen to you on my watch."

They were near her car. Mac had followed her out to Belmont Ridge, then trailed her back. "But what about you?" Jamie asked as she glanced over at his SUV. For an instant, she saw the smashed remains of Davis's truck. "What if something happens to you?"

"It won't," he said simply.

Cocky McGuire. "Despite what you might think, you're not some kind of indestructible powerhouse. None of the McGuires are. You can get shot, stabbed, *hurt*, just as easily as anyone else." And *that* was why she'd been avoiding his stare. Not out of fear but because of guilt. She'd agreed to stay in the area, but she hadn't agreed to pull someone else into the crosshairs of danger.

Not even someone who seemed to thrive on the risk.

"So, look, I—" Jamie broke off because she heard the sound of an approaching vehicle. The growl of tires. Someone was coming toward them, fast. She tensed just as a big, white SUV came rushing toward them.

She caught sight of the driver when the SUV braked to a quick stop about twenty yards away. "Davis?" She ran toward him. If he'd come all the way out there to find her, instead of just calling, then something must be wrong.

He opened the door and hurried to meet her.

"What happened?" She caught his arms. "Is everything all right? Did Henry come after you again?"

"Everything is fine." He looked around.

Nodded to Mac. "I just…I needed to talk to you in person. Before I left."

"Um, left?" She stepped closer to him. "Where are you going?" He'd been the one telling her to stay just hours before, and now he was leaving her? Her stomach clenched. *No, no, I can't be wrong. Not again—*

"Sean Nyle."

She stiffened at the name.

"He was the other lover, right, Jamie? The one that lasted a few months."

And as she stared up at him, Jamie's heart sank. *He knows.*

Chapter Seven

She glanced over her shoulder. Mac was close enough to overhear everything, but, well, Jamie figured if Davis had already uncovered her ex-lover's name, then all the McGuires would be learning this dark tidbit from her past, too. "Yes. He was the one."

"He told a court that you confessed to him, that you said—"

Jamie caught his arm. "Not out here, okay? Let's go inside." Because her clients could come up, and this wasn't the type of thing she wanted just anyone to overhear. It was humiliating enough as it was.

I wasn't just wrong about one lover. I had the terrible taste of choosing two men who hurt me.

Not saying another word, Jamie turned on her heel and headed inside the clinic. Sylvia looked up and gave a friendly smile. That smile dimmed a bit when she saw Jamie's face.

Sylvia jumped to her feet. "Is everything okay?"

Not even close. "Fine," Jamie said. "Just fine." She forced a smile. "Davis and I just need to have a quick talk." As she passed by Sylvia's desk, Jamie bent down and automatically rubbed Jinx's head. He usually hung out with them at the clinic, and just touching him for a moment made her feel better.

But when she entered her office, it wasn't only her and Davis. Mac had followed her inside, too. "Um, can you—" Jamie broke off. She'd been about to ask him to wait outside, but Mac was guarding her, so didn't he deserve to hear all of this, too?

She just… She wanted to keep some pride. She hated baring every bit of her pain to those men, even if Davis was her lover.

"Never mind," Jamie mumbled. She shut the door, sealing them all inside.

The little office was the only haven she had left. She had a few personal effects scattered around the room, and the picture of her and her brother—she'd tucked that into her top drawer. She'd get a new frame for it. She'd put it up soon. And remember what it was like to be loved so completely.

He never doubted me.

And she'd never doubted him.

Jamie paced to her desk. She didn't sit down behind it. Instead, she stopped in front of the desk, and she braced her hands on its surface. "What do you think you know?" Maybe she should have told him this part sooner, but she hadn't wanted Davis to doubt her. And Sean…he wasn't in the picture anymore. Not in any way. The situation didn't involve him, so she'd wanted to keep that particular skeleton shoved as far back in her closet as possible.

"I know you were involved with him, during your sophomore year of college."

Right. When she'd still been hurting. Still raw from losing her brother and desperate to fit in. She'd wanted to be like everyone else. All of the other students seemed happy. Normal.

But I wasn't like them. No matter how hard she'd tried to be.

"After it ended, he went to the Westports," Davis said. "In the documents I saw, he said he felt he had to share what you'd told him."

Hearsay. At least, that's what the legal term should have been but…

Money and power can do so much.

"You told him you were at fault." There was no emotion in Davis's voice or in his eyes. He was watching her, so carefully, and she wondered what he saw when he looked at her.

Her hands flattened against the desk.

Davis cleared his throat. "According to Sean Nyle, you confessed that you'd manipulated Henry. You were angry at your parents because they never paid any attention to you."

No, they hadn't. Her parents had barely noticed when she was home. Only Warren had noticed. They'd always been so close. Almost like Davis and Brodie. As long as she'd had Warren, she hadn't really cared that her father was always working or that her mother spent so many days with a wineglass close by.

"So you concocted this plan. You wanted to stage an attack, you wanted to make them notice you. You pushed Henry and told him how to get inside your house—"

"And I told him to stab me." Her hand lifted, sliding over her scrubs, over the scar on her left side. "I told him not to hit anything vital. I was already taking college-level biology courses in high school, prepping for my plans to be a doctor, so I knew just where he should cut me. I was never going to identity him, of course, just say that some masked attacker had hurt me." Even as she told this story, fury and disgust twisted through her. "I had it all planned out, but in the end, I changed my mind and decided to point the finger at Henry. To blame *him* when it had been my plan all along." At least, that was what Sean Nyle had stated. *But Sean was always such a liar.*

Jamie forced herself to hold Davis's stare. "And Henry was enraged when he found out that I'd turned on him. Poor, tormented Henry." Her cheeks felt numb. "He came looking for me at the university because he wanted to force me to admit what I'd done. But my brother—my trusting, foolish brother—believed my lies. He believed I was the victim. And Warren was caught in the middle when the gun went off. Accidentally, of course, because Henry never meant to hurt him. It wasn't his fault." Her chin lifted. "It was mine."

Davis gazed back at her. Still no emotion showed on his face. His eyes glittered at her. "That was Nyle's account of things."

Right. She glanced over at Mac. The McGuires were sure good at wearing those emotionless masks. She'd remember that. If only she could cut off her feelings that easily. After a tense moment, her focus returned to Davis. "And do you believe that story? Do you think I'm the crazy one? That I've been somehow playing you? What…do you think I staged the fire, the hit-and-run, the——"

Davis surged forward and caught her hands. "I want to hear *your* story."

Mac cleared his throat. "Think I'd like to be hearing it, too."

Others had heard it. They hadn't believed her.

She didn't want to talk with Mac there. She wanted to confide in Davis. He was the man she'd been with so completely the night before. And now...now he was the man staring at her with a stranger's gaze. So cold. Jamie shook her head. "Do you believe Sean Nyle's account?"

He didn't answer.

"I want to know." She'd held nothing back the night before. She'd never been so open with anyone. Maybe she was just destined to misjudge people. Maybe she'd been right to steer clear of deep friendships and lovers. She'd turned to veterinary science because animals...animals didn't hurt you. What you saw was what you got, and people—

"I want to hear *your* story," he said again.

She swallowed—twice—and managed to say, "Sean and I were friends for months. He knew who I was...everyone knew. I hadn't changed my last name then, and I hadn't run far enough away." Because the scholarship had been there, waiting for her. A scholarship she'd worked so hard to get. She'd still thought she could salvage part of her old life back then.

She'd been wrong.

"We became lovers."

A muscle flexed in his jaw. The only sign of emotion.

"A few months, that's all. I wanted to feel more with him, but I didn't." She'd started to worry that she couldn't feel anything for anyone, that her emotions had shut down because of Henry. *I was too afraid to feel.* "After we broke up, I thought we were still friends. I thought we had that, at least." Because it hadn't been some terrible vicious breakup. They'd both seemed to realize things weren't working. No drama. Just an end.

"Then later, I found out what he'd done." The betrayal had eaten right through her. "And I saw him on campus, driving a brand-new sports car. I learned that all of his tuition had been paid for the next four years, and I—I confronted him." Because the whispers had surrounded her. Gossip. Accusing stares. "He said he'd had a choice to make. That he hadn't hurt anyone...and that he hoped I understood." He'd stared at her as if she should *understand.* He'd seemed confused when she started crying, as if she truly didn't get that he hadn't hurt anyone.

"He's still locked up..." She whispered those words, and her throat actually hurt as she said them. "That's what he told me. 'He's still locked up. He won't get you. He's getting help.' As if the lies he'd told didn't matter. But they did matter. Because I knew Henry would get out sooner. He'd be free and he'd come for me." Her shoulders sagged. She felt so weary then. All the way to her bones.

Mac took a step toward her. "You're saying Henry's parents paid Sean to come forward with that tale?"

"I'm saying they paid him to lie. I'm saying they bought their son's freedom, again, and I knew that they wouldn't stop...not until my life—what was left of it—was destroyed. And my parents..." This hurt so much. It *gutted* her. "They backed up Sean's story. They said...they said they'd seen me acting out before, that they should have known..." She could still remember going into the prosecutor's office, not understanding *why* her parents would do that.

Everyone had turned on her.

So she'd left them behind.

Jamie looked down at her hands. "You know, I don't think I'd believe me, either."

Not once she'd said the story out loud. "My parents said I was responsible, my lover— both of them—they said I manipulated them. I wouldn't believe my story, either," she repeated. *My brother's blood was on my hands.* "I'd just walk away. It's the best thing." She looked up. "It's exactly what you should do. Just walk away from this mess." *From me.* "And don't look back."

He kept staring at her. *What do you see when you look at me?*

She tried to make her face as expressionless as his. Because when he left, she didn't want him to see how much it hurt her.

He should leave. It's better. It's—

"Go outside, Mac," Davis ordered.

Mac hesitated. "I don't think—"

"I need to talk with Jamie. Alone."

Now he wanted to talk alone? "I'm done talking." Done trying to convince him that she was innocent. The deck was stacked against her. When so much money and power was involved, why expect a different result?

She'd done some digging into Henry's life. She'd needed to know where he was, especially once he was released from the psychiatric facility.

She knew he was supposed to be some kind of model citizen now. That he spent millions on charity work. That he was slated to take over his father's company—

And I'll always see him as that wild-eyed boy who stabbed me, the monster in the dark. The monster who wouldn't stop no matter how much I begged.

Mac headed for the door. "I'm outside, if you need me."

Her gaze jerked to his face. He was staring at her…with sympathy?

"Just call," Mac said. Then he glared at Davis. "Watch your step, bro. *Watch it.*"

And Mac yanked open the door and left her alone with Davis.

Jamie didn't move. She was almost afraid to speak.

What now?

"STOP!" SULLIVAN RAN through the airport, and grabbed Grant's arm. His brother whirled toward him, frowning.

"Sully? What the hell?"

"I'm going to Connecticut." So what if that hadn't been the original plan? He'd changed his mind about their plan thirty minutes ago.

Because my brothers are right. I am changing. And I'm not sure I like the man I'm becoming.

Too much bitterness. Too much anger. Too much time spent longing for what he couldn't have.

"Since when?" Grant demanded as his gaze hardened. "You're supposed to be running down intel—"

"And I will, in Connecticut." Where he could get an up-close and personal look at the Westports. "I need to go, all right? Davis is swearing that Jamie is the victim, and I—" He shook his head. "I have to see for myself if he's right." He had to follow this case down the rabbit hole and see exactly where it went. "Stay with Scarlett." Because Grant had a woman who loved him, a woman who wasn't afraid of any darkness that Grant carried. "I've got this one, okay?"

Grant hesitated. "What have you been holding back from me?"

A mistake. One that Sullivan might have made because, hell, unlike Davis, he hadn't trusted the woman who'd come to him. He'd believed the other stories, instead.

Another time, another place.

"I need to get on that plane," Sullivan said.

Grant nodded. "Be careful."

"Aren't I always?"

"No, you aren't." Grant's brows lowered.

"You're running from demons, and we can all see it."

Maybe I won't run for much longer. Maybe I'll face them.

"It's been hard on everyone, I know," Grant continued. "The more we learn about our parents, about what happened to them... the more twisted the case becomes."

Yes, it did. Over the past few months, they'd made plenty of startling discoveries. They'd had friends—well, those friends had turned out to be enemies. A man who'd been like family to the McGuire's...he'd been revealed to be a traitor. There were so many secrets tied to the past, and some days, Sullivan wasn't sure if he even wanted to know the real truth. Maybe the truth wouldn't make their family stronger. Maybe it would tear them apart.

And that's why I've been keeping my secrets. I don't want to hurt my brothers or my sister. I've never wanted to hurt them.

But would they understand that? Or would they look at him with betrayal in their eyes?

He heard the announcement for the flight.

"Better go," Grant told him, voice gruff. "And be safe."

Sullivan nodded and hurried away. One

day, he'd have to tell his brothers and Ava the truth but…

That day wasn't today.

WHEN MAC LEFT the room—after giving Davis a final glare—Davis made sure to shut and lock Jamie's office door.

Tension had tightened every muscle in his body. There had been so much pain in Jamie's voice when she talked about her past. And *he'd* done that. He'd made her feel vulnerable. Exposed.

"I'm going to see Sean," Davis said as he turned to face her.

He caught Jamie's flinch.

"Why?" Jamie asked. "So he can tell you how much of a manipulator—"

"Because he's in Houston, and I think he could be the man behind the attacks."

"H-Houston?" Jamie paled and backed up a step. She bumped into the edge of her desk. "Since when?"

"Since six months ago. And I don't like that some jerk from your past is this close— not when these attacks are occurring. Coincidences like this don't just happen." He didn't buy it for a minute. "I wanted to hear all the details about what happened directly from you before I go."

She seemed to absorb this. "You wanted to see my face, to hear my voice…so you could decide if I was lying or telling the truth."

He didn't approach her. "You know I was a SEAL."

Jamie nodded.

"I've been in some of the most dangerous spots on earth." Places that he could never discuss. "I've captured international prisoners, and I've witnessed interrogation scenes…" He exhaled. "Well, let's just say that I learned to read people really well during my time working for Uncle Sam." He'd picked up on so much body language. Cues that had tipped him off to traitors. Signs that had shown him the guilty and the innocent.

"So…what?" Jamie asked him, her delicate brow furrowing. "You're some kind of lie detector? Is that what you're saying?"

"I'm saying that I can read people." Pretty damn well. After all, he'd been the first to notice Sully's lies. The secrets. And he'd had to tell the others.

We will learn what he's holding back.

And Sullivan was very, very good at keeping his mask in place.

"So you're reading me? Testing me?"

No, not a test—

Jamie marched toward him, her chin notched up in the air. "So, what's the verdict, then? Am I telling you the truth? Or are you just the latest in the line of men to fall for my lies?"

Her eyes were shooting blue flames. A flash of red stained her cheeks. She was angry, and he didn't blame her. He hated himself right then.

"I feel the exact way I felt before I walked into this office with you," he told her slowly. "Like you've been through too much. Like you've been hurt too much."

"What?" Her eyes widened. "You believe me?"

"You're not the kind of person who would get her lover to stab her six times. Who would just callously watch while her brother died."

Her lips trembled.

"I saw your face when you looked at his picture. I can hear the pain in your voice when you talk about the past."

She looked down, her gaze directed at her hands, as if she could see something on them.

Carefully now, he caught her chin between his thumb and forefinger. Davis tilted her face up so that she had to meet his gaze. "Let's be clear. I believe you."

"What if—" She broke off and cleared her

throat. "What if Sean just gives you more lies? Everyone else turned their backs on me." She shook her head. "I don't want you to look at me the way they all did."

I will never look at you that way.

Things were moving fast. Far faster than he'd realized, and he was falling—getting caught in Jamie's web. But not because of some manipulation or seduction. He wanted to be with her. "I won't."

"How can you be sure?" she whispered.

His fingers slid over the curve of her jaw. "Because I'm sure of you." He bent his head. Kissed her. He wanted to do a hell of a lot more than just kiss her, but he had to get on the road and get to Houston. "Stay at the guesthouse tonight. I'll be back." And soon. "Mac will keep an eye on you. You don't have to worry."

"I'm not worried about me." She searched his eyes and seemed to come to some conclusion. "I just want you to be safe. The last thing I want is for something to happen to you."

He smiled at her. "Sweetheart, I'm not an easy man to hurt." It would take a whole lot more than Sean Nyle to take him out.

Time for a little one-on-one time with the jerk.

THREE HOURS LATER, Davis braked in front of a newly constructed building. A new office, one that was still getting fresh sod set down outside.

Dr. Sean Nyle, Animal Care Hospital. There were only two cars in the lot. A slow day for the doctor. Davis took his time sauntering inside. The building was top of the line, filled with gleaming windows and decorative brick displays.

When he opened the door to the entrance, a pretty blonde looked up from behind the counter. "Welcome!" Then she frowned. "Do you... Where's your pet?"

He strolled to the desk. "I'm an old friend of Sean's, just in town for a little bit." He smiled at her. "I want to surprise him. Mind if I go back and say hi to my college roommate?"

She smiled back at him as she leaned conspiratorially forward. "He's in the last office on the right. I'm sure he'll be thrilled to see an old buddy."

Davis winked at her. "Oh, I bet 'thrilled' won't even come close to how he feels." He turned away from her and marched down the hall. Time to see the creep who'd helped to wreck Jamie's life.

A SOFT KNOCK sounded at Jamie's door. She flinched, then glanced up from the pile of paperwork on her desk. "Come in!"

The door opened, and Sylvia stood there. "Jamie...is everything all right?"

Jamie forced a smile. "Of course! Everything's fine." If fine happened to be a waking nightmare.

Sylvia shook her head. "Your house was destroyed in a fire. And don't think I didn't hear about the car accident."

She felt her smile dim a bit.

Sylvia shut the door. "Are we friends?"

"Yes, yes, of course!" Or... Sylvia was as close to a friend as Jamie had.

"Then, as your friend..." Sylvia exhaled. "I'm here, okay? If you need anything, if you want to talk..." Her head cocked to the right. "If you want to ease some of that burden you carry all the time and tell me what's really going on with you."

Jamie sucked in a sharp breath. "Sylvia, I—" *I don't want to tell you. I could barely tell Davis.* She tried to force her smile back in place. "I appreciate your concern, but I'm fine, really, I am."

Sylvia raised one brow and gazed doubtfully back at her.

"But thank you," Jamie added, meaning those words. "For caring enough to ask."

Sylvia nodded. She opened the door, slipped outside—

And Mac eased in.

Jamie frowned at him.

He shrugged. "I was eavesdropping. It's what I do."

Not the most polite thing to do.

"Got to keep you safe, so that means staying close." Now he shut the door.

She tensed, then tried to force her stiff muscles to relax.

"You don't have to face the world alone, you know."

Didn't she? "I've been facing things on my own for a very long time. I don't even know if I could do it differently now."

"You never know, until you try. You're expecting everyone to blame you. To shut you out. To judge. And some folks will do that."

He wasn't pulling any punches.

"I've seen it with my own family. With Ava. The looks and the gossip cut her to the quick." A faint growth of stubble lined his hard jaw. "But I've also seen good people step forward. I've seen people stand at her side. People can surprise you, so don't shut them all out before you see what they're really about." He gave her a little salute. "Now I'll be eavesdropping outside of your door if you need me."

Her lips had parted, but she wasn't sure what to say. Finally, the words came. "Mac!"

He glanced back at her.

"Is this about Sylvia?"

He shook his head. "Not just her. You thought Davis had already found you guilty, didn't you? So you held tight to your secrets. Better let those secrets go, before you lose something important."

Her heart slammed into her chest. "What if it's not mine to lose?" It couldn't be happening with Davis. Not so fast.

"Like I said, you never know—" he opened the door "—until you give people a chance."

She wanted to give Davis a chance.

She wanted to give him everything.

Chapter Eight

Davis threw open the door to last office on the right. "Sean Nyle!" he called out.

The guy behind the desk stared at him in confusion.

"Just the man I've been looking for," Davis growled, then he slammed that door shut behind him.

Sean jumped to his feet. He was a few inches shorter than Davis and about thirty pounds thinner. His blond hair glinted under the fluorescent light. "Who are you? And how'd you get back here?" He grabbed for the phone on his desk. "Did Candace let you back——"

Davis snatched the phone out of Sean's grasp. "Yes, Candace sent me back. So you and I could have a nice little chat." He smiled, and he knew the sight wouldn't be friendly. "I'm here to talk with you about a woman you knew years ago. A woman who went by the name of Jamie Bridgeton."

Sean blanched. "Get out! I don't have anything to say to you."

"Really? Huh, that's too bad. Because I've got quite a few things to say to you."

But Sean's jaw clenched. "I've already told you all everything I knew!"

You all? Interesting.

"I told you everything!" Sean snarled. "That was the deal. I tell you, you pay me and—"

"So you did get paid."

Sean blanched. "I… You…"

"I didn't pay you," Davis told him, anger churning inside of him. "Because I'm not working for the Westports."

All of the color bled from Sean's face.

"You sold her out, again. I suspected as much. I mean, you came down to Houston to escape that scandal up north…you had an affair with your partner's wife, right?" At least, according to the divorce papers he'd accessed. "You lost pretty much all your money in the divorce, and you needed some place to start fresh. You came down here and what? You found Jamie? You—"

"I will call the cops on you," Sean threatened. "Get out of my office. Get—"

"Someone burned down Jamie's house. A jerk ran her off the road. The truck she was in flipped four times."

Sean sagged and seemed to fall into the chair. "I…I didn't think they'd hurt her. They didn't hurt her before."

Rage burned inside of Davis. He stormed across the room and slammed his hands down on Sean's desk. "*Before*…you mean the first time you sold Jamie out? When you were paid by the Westports and you lied about her to everyone?"

"Lied…" Sean echoed. He was staring at his desk. The guy seemed dazed. "I…" He shook his head and looked up. "Who are you to Jamie? A lover?"

Yes. "I'm the guy she's hired to find out just who the hell is after her. And right now, my money is on you."

"No! I wouldn't hurt Jamie! I've never physically hurt her." Sean's Adam's apple bobbed. "We're friends. We have been for years. We've—"

"You told a Connecticut prosecutor that Jamie manipulated Henry Westport. That she tried to manipulate you. You told the court that she wanted attention from her parents. You told—"

"Stop!" Sean lifted his hand. Then he ran

that hand over his eyes. "I remember what I said, okay? Every single day, I remember." His hand dropped. "You're a PI, is that it? I guess I knew the truth would come out, one day."

It took all of Davis's self-control not to lunge across that desk and grab the guy. "You were paid to lie."

"I was paid to tell a story. That's what I did. I wasn't hurting anyone. Jamie wasn't going to be punished. Henry Westport was still going to get his counseling and I—" his lips lifted into a bitter smile "—I was going to be able to finish school. All my bills would be paid, easy as can be. I mean, all I had to do—"

"Was turn Jamie into a monster."

Sean's smile faded. "She hated me after that. Everyone in school…they heard. People would whisper about her. They keyed her car. Broke into her dorm room. They tormented her, and she hadn't done anything."

No, she hadn't.

"Jamie left after that. She just seemed to vanish. And I didn't see her again." Sean licked his lips. "Not until about six months ago. I was down here for a convention, and I happened to look up. Her hair is lighter, longer, but I'd know her anywhere. You don't forget a woman like her."

And you don't betray her, either.

"As soon as you saw her, you put in another call to the Westport family?"

Sean shoved to his feet. "No, no I didn't."

"Not right away, then." *Don't beat the hell out of him. Don't beat the hell out of him.* "But as soon as you realized you wanted to open a practice here? When you realized you needed an infusion of cash? You knew exactly where to go for that money. Just call the right person, offer the right information and boom—you get paid again." He hated the jerk in front of him.

"I didn't call them." Sean held his gaze. "I get it, you think I'm a piece of crap, and maybe I am, but I *didn't* call them. I didn't. Garrison showed up on my doorstep. He thought maybe I knew where Jamie was."

Henry's father. *"When?"* Davis thundered.

"A month ago."

Davis leaned across that desk. "So you didn't call then, but when Garrison showed up, you were only too happy to tell him what you knew."

"I needed the money," Sean whispered. "So, yes, dammit, I told him what I knew. I told him…" He shook his head. "And he paid me for my time."

"Blood money," Davis snarled. He lunged forward and grabbed the guy. His hands clenched around Sean's shirtfront. "That freak nearly killed her when she was seventeen. Why would you put her in the crosshairs again? Just for money?"

"No! It's not like that. Garrison said he wanted to make sure she was safe. *Safe!* I didn't tell Henry, and, besides, he's supposed to be different now. He's better. They fixed him at the clinic, he's—"

"If the father came looking for Jamie," Davis snapped out, "why do you think he was worried about her being *safe*? Maybe he knew his son was still hung up on her. He thought dear Henry might go after her again."

Horror blanched Sean's face. "I—I didn't know."

"Bull. You just didn't care. And now Jamie's lost her house, and she almost lost her life." He wanted to destroy the man in front of him. Instead, he forced himself to let the guy go. Davis took a step back. He could knock the fellow unconscious in an instant, and while that would feel good, it wasn't the right strategy.

Not for Jamie.

"The Westports aren't the only ones with connections. And Connecticut connections, they don't exactly fly down in Texas." He glared at the SOB. "I think you're going to find Houston very inhospitable from here on out. Not just Houston, but the whole state. If I were you, I'd pack up now." He inclined his head toward the guy. "Pack up and don't ever come near Jamie again."

"W-what? Are you threatening me? You can't! You—"

"I just did." Flat. Cold. "You made a mistake, and it's one I'll make sure you regret." He turned on his heel and headed for the door. He knew that Sullivan had been the one to fly up to Connecticut, not Grant, and he needed to get his younger brother on the line. Sullivan had to know about Garrison's visit and—

"You're involved with her, aren't you?"

His shoulders tensed.

"I can tell, just by the way you say her name."

Davis looked back at the guy. *Don't beat the hell out of him. Don't—*

"She gets under your skin, doesn't she?" Sean said. "That's what happened with me. She got close, and I didn't even realize it." He hesitated. "But Jamie, she won't feel the same way. She didn't with me. She won't with you. I don't think she can. Henry—the attack changed her. She's too closed off. I don't think she can love. I don't think she *wants* to love anyone."

Okay. So maybe he would beat the hell out of the guy. Davis rolled his wrists. "And that's one of the reasons you lied about her, isn't it? Because she dumped you, and you didn't take so well to rejection. So why not get back at her and make some cash at the same time?"

Sean staggered back a step. "No, no, I—"

But Davis had already crossed the room and shoved the guy back against the wall. "I'm an enemy you don't want. I have more connections than could you dream of." His voice was low, guttural. "I haven't spent the last ten years of my life in some office, screwing around when it suited me. I've been a SEAL. I've seen hell you can't imagine." He could feel the tremble shaking the man. "And if you ever do anything to hurt Jamie again, I will bring that hell to your door. I will give you nightmares that you can't escape, no matter how hard you try."

The door swung open behind them. "Dr. Nyle, I've got— *What's happening?*"

Ah, so the receptionist had just realized he wasn't an old friend.

"This won't be the last time you see me,"

Davis told him. "Because I'm going to make certain you're paid back for every bit of pain you gave to Jamie."

"I—I'm sorry—"

"Too late for that. You'd better just pray that jerk hunting her doesn't so much as bruise her skin. Because if something happens to her—" Davis stared into the guy's eyes and saw the terror blooming there "—you're done."

"Should I call the cops?" the receptionist squeaked.

"Yeah, do that." Davis shoved away from Sean. "And ask for Detective Carl Musata. He's a real close friend. I bet he'd just love to learn all about the doctor's close association to a murderer."

"What?" Now she wasn't squeaking. She was screaming.

Davis smiled at Sean. "I'll be seeing you." Then he stalked out, because if he didn't leave—right then—he might give in to his darker urges and take that guy down. And spending the night in lockup wasn't on his agenda. He wanted to get back to Jamie. He needed to get back to her.

When he marched out to his rental car, the sunlight hit him, far too warm for this time of the year. He yanked out his phone and had Sullivan on the line seconds later.

"Man, I just landed," Sullivan said. "Your timing is as good as always—"

"Henry's father has been looking for Jamie." He couldn't keep the fury out of his voice. As quickly as possible, he filled Sullivan in on the details of how Sean had found Jamie *and* about how the guy had sold her out again. "Nyle handed over her new name," he finished, the words curt. "He just gave her up."

And from there, hell, Garrison wouldn't have even needed to hire his own PI. A simple internet search would have led him right to Jamie.

"Why is the father after her?" Sullivan asked. "I thought the son was the one with the obsession."

Davis slid into his car. "Sean said the guy was *worried* about her."

Sullivan swore. "You think Garrison knew his son was still fixated on her."

Yes. "I think I want to know exactly where Henry Westport is right now. I want you to get eyes on him." And he wanted to get back to Jamie, as fast as he could. "I'm going to call Mac. I need him to stay with her. This mess is a powder keg, and the last thing I want…" He exhaled heavily. "I don't want it to explode on her."

JAMIE HAD A new lover. A man who seemed desperate for her. A man who was used to violence.

A man who was in his way.

Davis McGuire thought he was indestructible. All of the McGuires seemed to think they were a cut above everyone else.

They were wrong. They were human. They could be hurt. They could bleed. They could die. Just like everyone else.

The hit-and-run had been a mistake. He should have stayed there and finished the man off. But he hadn't expected Davis to recover so quickly.

I won't be caught off guard again.

This time, he'd be better prepared.

He would learn Davis's weakness. Learn all of the weaknesses for the McGuires...because Jamie had brought the whole family into their web. She was trying to get her protectors lined up, but it wouldn't matter if she had an army at her side.

He'd found her, and she wasn't going to get away. She was going to suffer. She would pay for everything that she'd done. She wouldn't get away scot-free.

Not this time. Not ever again.

Jamie was so good at luring men to her. So good at playing the innocent. But he'd learned the truth about her over the years. She was a liar. She didn't care about anyone or anything but herself.

She certainly didn't care about her new lover. She was using him, just as she'd used the other one. So many people thought Jamie was innocent, perfect. A victim.

She was so much more.

And she's mine.

Every wicked inch of her.

"ARE YOU SURE you're all right?" Mac asked as he hesitated near the front of the guesthouse. He was standing on the narrow porch, his gaze on Jamie.

She smiled at him. Despite his fierce reputation, Mac was pretty sweet, she thought. He'd been a silent shadow for most of her day, and, yes, he looked rather intimidating—she thought it would be hard for an ex-Delta Force guy like him to look exactly warm and cuddly, but he'd been more than a perfect gentleman. "I'm fine." Jamie gestured around her. "I've got the security of the McGuire ranch. How could I not be safe?"

The porch light shone down on them, and she saw the sadness flicker over his face. "Not even being out here can keep everyone safe."

She hadn't talked with Davis a lot about his parents, but she knew how much their death had hurt the entire McGuire clan. She could see the pain on Mac's face. "I'm sorry," Jamie said. "So sorry about what happened to your parents."

His smile was bittersweet. "You always think there is plenty of time for things. Later. You can say the things you meant to say... *later.* Do the things...later. But what if later doesn't come?"

Her arms wrapped around her stomach. There had been so much she'd wanted to tell her brother, and she never got the chance. "I heard that a few months ago... Ty Watts was arrested." That story had sure dominated the news for a while. Ty had been Mark Montgomery's ranch foreman, his right-hand man. The guy had also been stalking Ava. Ty had been obsessed with the woman for years, and he'd been determined to take her away from Mark. *Even if he had to kill Ava in order to do it.*

She'd been transfixed by the story because she'd understood—too well—the fear and horror Ava must have felt.

His face hardened. "The creep is locked up, where he belongs."

"Is it true..." She fumbled, not wanting to

be a gossip, but the question wouldn't stay quiet. "Was he out here the night your parents were killed? Did he really see the men who attacked them?" Because that had been the rumor. Ty had offered to give up the killers, in exchange for a deal.

A deal the McGuires hadn't wanted to accept.

"Ty Watts is a liar and a killer. You can't believe the things that he says." His lips thinned. "Yeah, he was spouting that story, but we had...connections we could use to check him out."

"Connections?"

"His cell mate."

Her brows rose.

"For the right money," Mac told her, "you can get people to do anything."

Jamie shivered. She knew his words were true. Money had exchanged hands, and her life had crumbled.

"He's been with Ty for a while now, and so far, it's looking like Ty's story is pure bull. Just his desperate attempt at leverage. He said he was at the ranch, watching Ava—always watching her—but he has no concrete evidence to give us about that night, and the *last* thing we would do is bargain with that guy when our sister's safety is on the line."

Right. Because that mattered to the Mc-Guires. For an instant, Jamie thought of her own parents. Her mother's gaze had seemed so accusing at Warren's funeral. Jamie had been numb that day. As she'd watched his casket slowly lower into the ground, Jamie had felt as if she'd died, too. Her body had been leaden, and she'd just stayed there, helpless to walk away.

Her father and mother had left her there. Everyone had left.

And then, so much later, when the US Marshal had appeared, offering her a chance at a new life, he'd told her that she would have to leave on her own. That she'd have to cut the connections to her family.

What connections?

I took his offer. I didn't look back.

Or, at least, she hadn't, not until the past came looking for her.

"Have a good night, Jamie," Mac told her as he gave a little salute. Then he turned away.

"Have you heard from Davis?" Because she hadn't. She'd thought of calling him, but if he was still with Sean...

Mac glanced back at her. "Yes." There was a new, tense note in his voice.

"He's okay, then?"

"He's on his way back to you."

Her shoulders slumped a bit. She hadn't even realized they were tight.

"He has some things he needs to tell you," Mac continued in that same slightly stilted voice. It was a voice that told her he already knew exactly what Davis wanted to talk with her about—and he didn't think Jamie was going to like what Davis had to say.

She stared at him, and, with a sinking heart, she knew.

Sean sold me out again.

Some people never changed.

"Good night," Mac told her again.

She stepped back. Closed the door. Made sure she locked it securely. But she didn't head for the bedroom. She grabbed her laptop—a new one that Sylvia had picked up for her—and booted up the machine. Then she went right back to the search that had consumed her whenever she'd had a free moment at the clinic.

A search for Henry Westport. The world was such an open book now, thanks to the internet. You could learn so much about a person. You could take a glimpse right into someone's life.

I want to see your life, Henry. I want to see where you are. What you're doing.

Because some people never truly did

change. And some people, some people just became even more twisted with the passage of time.

SULLIVAN STARED AT the Westport estate. A huge, sprawling place. One that shouted old money and power. Guards were positioned at the main gate. He'd already counted four security cameras. If you wanted in that place, then you definitely had to announce your presence and get the official invitation.

Or else you'd just get kicked to the curb.

Henry Westport was supposed to be inside that estate. So far, Sullivan had seen no sign of the man at all. Not of Henry…and not of Henry's father, Garrison.

But the night was young, and he wasn't about to go anywhere, not until he'd laid eyes on Henry. He wanted to see for himself if Henry was truly up in Connecticut…

Of if you're down in Texas, terrorizing Jamie.

He settled in, got comfortable, and he made his plans.

A FAINT KNOCK sounded at her door. Jamie's head whipped up, and she blinked blearily. She'd been staring at that computer screen for hours. She'd gotten lost, reading articles, digging into old news stories…and now Jamie saw that it was nearing midnight.

The knock came again. Faint. She rose to her feet and crept toward the door.

"Jamie, it's me."

Her creep turned into a hurried rush as she recognized Davis's voice. She flipped the locks and yanked open the door.

He filled the doorway. Big and strong and—Davis. She was so happy to see him that she didn't even hesitate. She just threw her arms around him and held tight. "I'm glad you're back."

He stiffened against her, and Jamie realized—oh, no, maybe it was too much. Or maybe he'd learned something from Sean, some lie that had made him doubt her. She tried to pull back.

But his arms locked around her, and he held her even more tightly. "Glad to be back."

And she felt warm. Good.

Happy.

I missed him. He was only gone for hours, but I missed him.

They made it fully into the guesthouse, and Davis shut the door. His gaze slid around the room, lingering on her new laptop. The screen was up, and it was easy to view the title of the article she'd been reading.

Westport Heir Overcomes Dark Past.

"Everyone likes a comeback story," she said, shifting a bit nervously from foot to foot. "At least, that's what I've heard." The reporter had certainly been impressed by Henry. She'd talked about his struggles, but never specifically mentioned just *why* Henry had wound up receiving psychiatric counseling. The reporter had glossed over that whole murder and stalking bit.

"You might want to sit down," Davis told her.

Why? She already knew he wasn't about to tell her good news. "I'm fine standing." Then Jamie shook her head. "Look, just tell me. Whatever it is, I can handle it. Really." She knew someone was after her. She knew—

"He sold you out again."

Right.

She'd known that, too.

"Sean Nyle has a new office, a fancy new car…"

Oh, she'd seen him with a fancy car once before.

"And he told me that he saw you a few months back. At a convention in Houston."

Her heart sank at that news. She hadn't seen him. She'd thought she was safe attending a regional event. She'd thought, *Maybe I don't have to hide so long, all the time.* She'd been wrong.

"According to Sean, Garrison Westport sought him out about a month ago. He wanted to know about you, and Sean told him everything he knew."

"For the right price," Jamie mumbled. And to think, she'd once believed they were friends. She'd thought that Sean cared about her. "Do you know—" now she turned from Davis and began to pace "—how much it hurts to know I was so wrong about someone, twice?" Sure, Sean hadn't come after her with a knife, but he'd been more than willing to throw her under the bus or to offer her up to a killer. And her parents had done the same thing. "Why?" Jamie asked. "Why don't I matter?"

That was a question that her seventeen-year-old self had wondered too many times, and she hadn't meant to blurt those words out. They were her secret shame. Her pain. Her—

He caught her arm and spun Jamie around to face him. "You do matter. Sean...he doesn't. He's a piece of crap who isn't worth your time. You matter, Jamie. You're good and smart and strong. You matter a whole damn lot."

Her breath caught as she searched his eyes.

"I've spent years being obsessed," he said. "Consumed with the desire to find the people who killed my parents. I didn't think past that point. Didn't even try to move on…and then I saw you. Walking to the stables. The sun shining on your hair."

She couldn't have spoken then if her life depended on it.

"Things started to change for me. And the more I learned about you, the more I kept changing. I didn't want my life to just be about the dead any longer."

And she didn't want her life to just be about fear.

"I wanted to get to know you. I wanted to be with you." His fingers slid down her arm in a light caress that made goose bumps rise on her skin. "That's still what I want. *You* matter, Jamie. You matter so much, to me." His face was intense, his gaze warm with emotion.

For the first time in longer than she cared to remember, Jamie felt a stirring of hope inside her chest. Hope that maybe things could be different for her. "I wish I'd met you a long time ago."

"You have me now, and, sweetheart, I'm not going anyplace."

Neither was she. Jamie stared into his gaze

and made that decision. No more running. No more hiding. She wasn't going to keep looking over her shoulder. She'd face the threat out there. She'd overcome it. And she would be happy.

Because Davis was right there with her, offering her a glimpse of the future—a future she wanted. A life that she could have. One that wasn't about fear and the pain from betrayals long past.

One that was about something fresh.

Something that might be love?

Her gaze slid to his lips. Sensual lips. He'd kissed her, stroked every inch of her, and he'd given her so much pleasure that her body had quaked. She wanted that again. She wanted him again. So she reached up, wrapped her arms around his neck, and she kissed him. She poured all of her passion into that kiss, all of the emotions that she felt but couldn't name.

And the heat was there, flaring between them. Rising to engulf her because when they touched, when they kissed, the electric connection surged between them.

She could wish they'd met sooner. She could wish her life had been different.

Or she could just enjoy being in the moment with him.

Her tongue slid over the curve of his lower lip. Then she bit that lip, a light, sensual tug, and when he growled, she smiled.

"I'm glad you're back with me," Jamie told him. *And I'm not going anywhere. Not anymore.* Together, they'd face the challenges that came their way.

He pulled her closer. Her toes brushed over his boots. She wore a pair of jogging pants and a T-shirt, and he had on his jeans and a dark shirt, a shirt that made his skin appear even more golden, his hair darker.

The guy looked good in black.

But she eased back. Her hand slid down his body until she was just touching his left hand. Then Jamie turned and began walking toward the bedroom. She kept her grip on his hand, tugging him lightly. She knew exactly what she wanted that night—and it wasn't to spend more time pouring over articles about a monster from her past.

She wanted Davis.

So when they entered the bedroom, she started to strip. Her fingers didn't tremble, and she met his gaze as she tossed aside her shirt, then her bra. She didn't feel self-conscious at all as she stood before him. He didn't mind her scars. She wasn't even sure he saw them when he looked at her.

His eyes were darkening with desire. His breath coming a little rougher.

His desire was a heady thing. He made her feel beautiful. Powerful.

She pushed the jogging pants—and her underwear—down her legs. She stood before him, completely naked. Her breasts thrust toward him, her hands stayed loosely at her sides.

And his gaze raked over her. She could feel that hot gaze of his like a caress on her body. Stroking her. Teasing her. Turning her on.

She stepped toward him. Jamie put her hands on his chest. Her fingers slid down, and she pushed up his shirt so that she could touch his skin. *So strong.* She loved the ripple of his muscles beneath her fingers. She pushed the shirt higher and pressed a kiss to his chest. Then her lips feathered over his nipple. She licked. She—

"I thought about you every moment on the drive back from Houston." His voice was a rough rumble. "I couldn't get back to you fast enough. I needed to see you." His hands locked around her hips. "Touch you."

"You're touching me now," she whispered back. She wanted him to touch her more. To touch her everywhere.

Would it be as good this time? They'd been

so frantic for each other before. Would it be the same way? Could it still be as good?

He kissed her. His tongue slid into her mouth even as he pulled her closer against him. His arousal pushed against her, heavy and hard.

"I want to touch you more," he growled and then they were rushing back, moving in a tangle of limbs until they crashed on the bed. "I want you wild."

She was on her way to being wild. Jamie didn't even try to hold on to her control. She helped him, shoving away his clothing so that she could feel him, skin to skin. All of him.

He stroked her.

She kissed him.

He made her moan.

She slid down his body. Explored him with her hands and mouth, and she made him growl.

Her breath panted out as she straddled his hips. He was so big and strong, but she wasn't afraid of Davis. Not even a little bit. Maybe she should have been afraid.

I'm not. Not of him. Never of him.

She helped him put on the protection. Then Jamie arched her hips, taking just the tip of his arousal into her. Sliding against him, rocking her hips, savoring the moment.

"Sweetheart, I need *everything* from you."

He tumbled her back, and Jamie found him above her, caging her, surrounding her. He drove deep, filling her in one hard thrust, and her body arched into his. With every moment, the passion seemed to blaze hotter, the need twisted tighter, and she couldn't hold anything back. She didn't want to hold back. Her legs wrapped around his hips, and she slammed up to meet him, again and again. His hand pushed between their bodies, and he stroked her, right at the center of her desire.

Jamie didn't just shudder in pleasure then. She exploded. She bit his shoulder, trying to muffle her scream because the climax was that good. Enough to make her go wild as she shuddered and gasped beneath him. A release that kept rolling through her, strong and hard and—

"You're so beautiful...you feel so good..." He kissed her neck. Held her tighter. Thrust deeper. "Can't...let...you...go..."

And he was with her. She could feel the jerk of his hips, and when he lifted his head, she saw the pleasure streaking across his face.

Better than last time. Stronger.

Hotter.

Sweat slickened their bodies. Her heart raced.

And she arched up to him again.

I CAN FEEL HIM, inside and out. He surrounds me.

Jamie stared up at the darkened ceiling. Her body was completely sated. She was pretty sure she'd be sore the next day, but she didn't care. She felt good.

Happy.

There it was again, that sneaky emotion, creeping up on her.

She smiled, and her eyelids began to sag. It was good to be wrapped up in his arms. To have him close—

Her eyes flew open. "You should...you should go up to the main house."

His fingers trailed over her shoulder. "Why? Do you want me to leave?"

"I..." No, she wanted him to stay. "I might have the dreams again." Nightmares. She didn't want to scream when he was near.

"If you do, I'll be here."

A lump rose in her throat.

"Dreams can't hurt you."

"They're not just dreams." If only. Nightmares were just whispers that faded when the darkness ended.

What happens when the darkness doesn't end?

"I'll be here," he said again.

And she knew he wasn't worried about

nightmares or memories. She wasn't sure if anything scared Davis McGuire.

So she let her eyes close. She'd warned him. And if he wanted to stay with her...

A faint smile curved her lips. Then she wanted to be with him.

Chapter Nine

Sullivan's footsteps were swallowed by the lush carpeting as he headed into Westport Industries. As luck would have it—luck, or perfectly planned timing—Garrison Westport was just striding across the lobby.

"Ah, Garrison…" Sullivan called out. "Just the man I was hoping to see."

Garrison—and his entourage of men in suits—turned at Sullivan's call.

Sullivan smiled at them. He'd worn his own suit today, though he usually hated the things. But he'd wanted to fit in, or at least, get past security.

"Do I know you?" Garrison asked with a frown.

"You will," Sullivan promised.

Garrison gave him a polite smile. "Why don't you talk to my assistant? Oliver can schedule a sit-down for—"

"We share a mutual acquaintance," Sullivan said. "Sean Nyle sent me."

That polite smile froze on Garrison's face.

"I just need a few moments of your time." Sullivan pointed toward the elevator. "How about we go up and have a little one-on-one chat?" He offered the man his own polite smile, though he had been told his grin rather resembled a shark's.

Garrison wiped his brow. *Sweating already?*

"Sir, I'll take care of this man," one of the suits said with authority. Ah, would that be Oliver? The assistant was aiming high.

But Garrison waved the younger man away. "I've got this. Yes, yes…" he said as he inclined his head toward Sullivan and hurried into the elevator. "Let's have that little chat."

Sullivan followed him.

When the suit—Oliver?—tried to follow, Sullivan put his hand on the man's chest. "Sorry, I'm afraid this is a private meeting." He pushed Oliver back. "Catch the next ride."

The elevator doors closed on Oliver's stunned face.

"I don't know what Sean Nyle has told you," Garrison snapped, "but I simply made a charitable donation to the boy's college fund years ago because I appreciated his honesty and—"

Sighing, Sullivan leaned forward and pressed the button to stop the elevator.

"Wh-what are you doing?" There was a slight break in Garrison's otherwise pompous voice.

Sullivan crossed his arms over his chest and turned to face Garrison. "Exactly what I told you before. Having a private chat with you. Your suits are no doubt rushing upstairs, and I don't want to deal with their crap. So I thought we'd just have our little chat right here."

Garrison's mouth was opening and closing, fishlike. For a moment, Sullivan just studied the older man. Garrison was in his early sixties, but his hair was still a dark brown. Only the faintest of wrinkles marked the man's face. He could easily have passed for someone half his age.

He was fit, tall and currently…sweating. A lot.

But fear could do that to a man.

"Who are you?" Garrison demanded.

"I'm a man who knows what you've done." *Always make the suspect think you know more than you do.* He'd learned that from an Austin police detective he'd once thought was a good friend. Too late, he'd learned that Shayne had betrayed him.

But that was another story. For another twisted day.

So much betrayal. How do you ever know who to really trust?

"I haven't done anything," Garrison blustered. "I haven't—"

"You recently had a meeting with Sean Nyle in Houston, Texas. You paid him to tell you everything he knew about Jamie Bridgeton." There was no point in beating around the bush. The guy already knew exactly where Jamie was, so mentioning her now wouldn't make her any more or any less of a target.

Garrison's eyelids flickered. "I have no idea what you're talking about."

Sullivan rolled his eyes. "Do I look as if I want to hear your bull? You told him you were worried about her safety, and then you plunked down a big chunk of change to find out where she was."

"That didn't happen!"

Sullivan lifted one brow. "Maybe I should just call a reporter I know." He didn't know any reporters in Connecticut. "See what she thinks about the situation and the money trail you left behind when—"

"I had to stop the woman from harassing my family!"

Harassing *them*?

"I was worried she'd be a threat," Garrison nodded. "So I had to find out where she was. Because if the harassment hadn't stopped, I would have stopped *her*."

The guy had just threatened Jamie...*right in front of me*. It was a good thing Sullivan had come for the little chat. He could only imagine how well Davis would have just taken that statement.

"The notes started coming to my home... packages that I knew she must have sent." Garrison glared at Sullivan. "The past is dead. She needs to let it go."

"What notes?"

"I won't forget." Garrison bit out the words. *"Money doesn't buy forgiveness."*

Interesting.

"The notes started coming to my house— with dead flowers, dead roses. I tracked the florist, and he told me that a blonde woman had ordered them. A blonde who paid in cash."

"And you figured that blonde had to be Jamie. Cause there aren't any other blonde women your son has terrorized."

Garrison looked away.

Or are there more women? Hell.

"I wanted her to stop. I wanted her to leave me alone."

There was something in the guy's voice... "But then you found out Jamie was all the way down in Texas. When you learned that, you had to see she wasn't the one who'd been sending you the notes." *If* any notes had even been sent. Because he wasn't buying the guy's story. Not at all.

Garrison's lips clamped shut.

"You flew back into town this morning," Sullivan said. "Private flight..." Because he'd bribed the guy's driver and gotten that information. "So I am very curious...just where have you been?" *Down in Texas, making Jamie's life hell?*

It was sure looking like he'd been wrong about Jamie. Davis had been right, and he knew his brother wasn't going to let him forget that anytime soon.

"None of your damn business." Sullivan glared at him. "Start this elevator or I will have you arrested, I will—"

"Her home was torched. A hit-and-run driver slammed into her." *Slammed into my brother.* "So you can see where I'd be a little curious. I mean, you knew where she was.

You were in Texas a month ago, and now, these *incidents* have started to happen."

For just a moment, fear flashed in Garrison's eyes. "She's…all right?"

"Where. Were. You?"

"Business trip. I had to go check on a factory down in New Orleans."

"I can verify this, you know."

Garrison's gaze cut away from him. "Then verify it."

"Where's your son?"

Garrison actually backed up a step.

"According to his assistant, he's here," Sullivan continued. "Working hard. But…that's not true, is it? Because I already checked today. From the look of things, Henry hasn't been in to work for quite a while. The mail has certainly stacked up on his desk."

"Leave my son alone!"

"Maybe your son should leave Jamie alone."

Garrison swiped his forehead again. "It's not what you think! He's not— He's not in Texas!"

"Then where is he?"

Garrison huffed out a hard breath. "You're her friend? Her lover? She sent you here to threaten me—"

"I haven't threatened you. I've asked you

questions. The cops are involved in Texas. They're investigating the attacks, and they will follow the trail right back to you." The McGuires would make sure of it. "This time, he's not a kid, and you won't be able to buy your way out of the hell he's made."

"He didn't do it!" Garrison's cheeks flushed dark red. "He's...he's back in the clinic, all right? There was a break—after he found one of those notes that *she* sent. He started talking about her again. Got obsessed, all over again. Only Henry realized what was happening this time. He checked himself into that clinic. He's getting help. So, no, he's not down there, stalking her." His hands were shaking as he straightened his suit. "He's at Grace Meadows, trying to hold on to his sanity once again. That woman has always had a dark pull on him. She plays with his head, and she makes him do things—"

"You don't even believe that crap, so stop spouting it." *Grace Meadows.* He knew his next stop.

Garrison lunged forward and pushed the button to get the elevator moving again.

Sullivan just watched him. He'd learned what he needed, for the moment. As soon as the elevator doors opened, Garrison leaped out and yelled, "Security!"

Sullivan shook his head. "I'm already gone." But he pointed toward Garrison. "Though I do think I'll be seeing you again."

Garrison paled.

The doors slid closed.

THE HOUSE WAS a total loss. Jamie stared at the charred remains of her home. She didn't have any appointments until the afternoon, so she'd wanted to go and see her home.

What was left of it.

Davis had come with her. He'd warned her that it wasn't going to be easy, and he was right. Seeing the house like that—gutted...

I can just start over. I can make a new home.

"Right. No, no, you tell me exactly what you find at Grace Meadows," Davis said.

His words drew her gaze away from the blackened house—and the two lone walls that remained standing. Davis was on his phone, pacing a few feet away.

"Confirm it, Sully. See him for yourself. Yes, I'll talk with you then." He hung up and pushed the phone back into his pocket.

When he looked over at her, Jamie tensed. *Sullivan is in Connecticut, but Henry isn't. He's out here, he's—*

"Sully just talked with Garrison Westport. The man admitted to seeing Sean. To getting information on you." His jaw clenched. "But so far, there's no sign of Henry. According to his father, Henry checked himself into a psychiatric clinic called Grace Meadows. The family is keeping it quiet, but he's supposedly been there for weeks."

She rubbed her chilled arms and glanced around. "If he's not there…"

Then Henry is here, watching me. Hunting me.

"Sullivan will know for certain soon. He's on his way to the clinic now."

She glanced back toward her house's remains. Jinx had loved playing near the trees in the back.

"Jamie, have you had any kind of contact with the Westports? I mean, since you—"

"I haven't spoken with them in eight years." Not that she'd counted the days. "Not since I asked Garrison Westport what he thought would happen when Henry's 'therapy' was over."

Sean had just sold her out. Garrison had been so smug as he'd stared down at Jamie.

My son's life won't be ruined by a mistake.

She'd been confused…had she been the mistake? Had her brother's death been the mistake?

"Counseling and medicine…I know they

can work wonders," Jamie said. "But I also know that Henry Westport told me that he'd never let me go. That he would find me. That he would never stop. And I believed what he said. I believed that when he got out, he would come after me."

And he had.

She headed toward the trees. The man on the motorcycle had been hiding behind those trees that first night. If she'd come back alone, would she have been found the next day? Her ashes part of the charred wreckage that remained in the aftermath?

"I checked with the cops this morning," Davis said as he followed behind her. "The car that hit us was stolen. They're searching it for evidence now, but I'm not holding out much hope they'll find anything we can use. When I saw that guy at the wreck, he was wearing black gloves."

Yes, she remembered that. Black gloves and a ski mask. "I couldn't see his eyes," Jamie said as she stared into the woods.

"What?"

"It was too fast. I—I just had an impression of the black gloves, reaching out to me. The gloves and the ski mask. I didn't even look at his eyes." There would have been eye holes in the ski mask. "If I'd seen his eyes, I would have known for sure." She turned toward him. "But it has to be Henry. No one else would want to do this to me. I—I haven't gotten close to anyone." *Only to Davis.* "I haven't slipped up. No one would want to hurt me, no one—"

He pulled her into his arms. "You didn't do this. It's not your fault, none of it. I don't care what BS the Westports spewed, none of this is on you."

Her arms wrapped around him. She held him tight. Over his shoulder, she could see the wreckage of her home and—

"Someone's coming," Jamie said, tensing. A blue SUV was heading down her driveway. Moving slowly. Almost silently.

Davis pulled away from her and turned toward the vehicle.

"The fire marshal?" Jamie asked. "Is that him?"

"No, Quint drives a county truck." He paced toward the SUV. She could see the sudden, battle-ready tension in his body. "I'll be damned. I *told* him to stay away."

What?

But then Davis was hurrying toward the vehicle. The driver had braked, and he was pushing open his door. Stepping out into the sunlight. She could see his hair and the sharp angles of his face…a *familiar* face.

Ice water poured through her veins.

"Sean?" His name came from her as a sharp denial because, no, he couldn't be standing there.

But he heard her cry. His head turned toward her. For an instant, he actually smiled.

She shook her head.

And Davis drove his fist into the guy's jaw.

SULLIVAN PARKED IN front of Grace Meadows. When he'd called Davis, he'd already been close to his destination. Rolling green hills surrounded the place—it looked like a scene from a damn movie.

The first thing he noticed—well, after those hills—was that there was no security. At least, no security guards. Security cameras were perched around the perimeter, but those would be easy enough to bypass.

If someone wanted to get out.

He'd done some fast and frantic digging on the place before this little visit. Grace Meadows was a residential facility—a *voluntary* facility. That meant the patients weren't secured there. They could come and go as they pleased.

Has Henry been coming and going...all the way down to Texas? He hadn't found a record of Henry flying down to Texas, but with all the Westport money, it would be easy enough for the guy to cover his trail.

A little flirting at the front desk gave him a quick entrance to the facility. And to Henry's corridor. He strolled across that gleaming tile. Flowers were everywhere. People smiling. Giant TVs were on the walls. This place wasn't like any psych ward he'd ever seen before.

Then he turned toward Henry's room.

And he found a man standing guard. *Interesting.*

The man lifted his hand. "Mr. Westport doesn't want visitors."

"I'm not a visitor." Sullivan smiled. "I'm a counselor."

"No, you're not." The guy, all three hundred pounds of him, went into a menacing pose. "You're an unwanted guest, Mr. McGuire, and you need to leave."

Well, well...so Garrison had put out his guard dogs. He'd known that Sullivan would head to Grace Meadows, and he'd wanted to make sure that there was no chance Sullivan could talk to Henry.

Did the guy really think this would slow me down? A minor annoyance, that was all.

Besides, Sully had already anticipated this situation.

He glanced at his watch. *Five, four, three, two...*

The fire detector shrieked, the blast truly earsplitting.

"That means we all have to get out of here," Sullivan murmured helpfully when the body of bulk didn't move. "Better grab Westport and run, because if he even gets a little smoke inhalation, I'm guessing you won't get paid."

The guy glanced over his shoulder. That was the moment Sullivan needed. He shoved against him, and they both went crashing in. The man inside the room yelled and jumped to his feet.

"Well, hello there, Henry..." Sullivan began, but then his eyes widened. *"What the hell?"*

"I TOLD YOU to never come near her!" Davis yelled.

Sean staggered back and slammed into the side of the SUV.

"I told you to stay away, and you track her down. You come to her home?" He lifted his hand. "You—"

"Stop it!" Jamie grabbed Davis's hand and held on tight. "What are you doing? *Stop!*"

He turned to look at her and found Jamie staring at him in horror.

"You can't attack him," Jamie said. Her gaze was stark. "This isn't you!"

Yes, sweetheart, it is. I will attack anyone who tries to hurt you. She'd heard about his dark side before, but this was the first time she'd seen it.

"Do you just…attract violent men…Jamie?" Sean asked, grunting.

Davis started to hit him again.

"Stop," Jamie said. "He's not worth this." Her fingers had wrapped around his arm.

Davis glared at the man before him. Blood dripped from Sean's lip—he'd busted that lip. The guy had gotten off lightly. Very, very lightly.

"I— Hell, I wanted to make sure she was all right!" Sean swiped away the blood that was dripping down his chin. "I wanted to see if the story you were spinning was real or not, and I—" He broke off as his gaze slid to the black remains of Jamie's home. "Hell, I didn't want it to be true." His shoulders slumped. "I needed it to be a lie."

Davis slowly lowered his hand. "You drove all this way…"

"Because I had to know." Now Sean's blood-covered chin jutted into the air. "I had to know if I'd done this. If I'd made her a target." Then he looked over at Jamie. "I'm sorry. So damn sorry."

Jamie didn't move.

"God, you still look the same," Sean whispered. "Still just as beautiful, and you still hate me just as much, don't you?"

Davis stepped in front of Jamie. "You sent them after her. *You* led the guy right to her door!"

"I needed the money! I had nothing, *nothing*! And I didn't think Garrison would hurt her. Garrison never hurt her. He just wanted to look after his son, and I—I did some checking." He rushed to the left, trying, no doubt, to make eye contact with Jamie. But Davis just moved, too, deliberately blocking him. He didn't want Sean even looking at her. "Henry is different! Better! He hasn't hurt anyone! He's on a dozen charity boards, and he's—"

"He killed my brother," Jamie said, her voice trembling. "And he tried to kill me. You *know* what he did."

Davis hated the pain in her voice. He didn't take his eyes off Sean. He was just waiting,

waiting for Sean to push him so that Davis could attack.

But Sean staggered away from the SUV. He headed toward the shell of Jamie's house, and he just stared at it, as if he couldn't quite believe his eyes.

"All I did…" He kept looking at the ash on the ground. "I just…I said I'd seen you at a vet convention. You had a different last name. You were in Texas. I—I did some checking at the event. I learned you were living just outside Austin and I told him that. But the guy has so much money. So many connections— I figured he could have found out all of that information on his own! Either I told him and made a little extra cash, or someone else would have found you for him."

Davis glanced over at Jamie. Her skin was so pale. He wanted to wrap her in his arms and hold her tight.

"How much?" she asked as she took one step, then another, toward Sean. "How much was my life worth this time?"

Sean spun toward her. *"I'm sorry!"*

And the guy ran to her.

Oh, the hell he did.

Just before Sean could reach her, Davis stepped into his path, and he knocked the jerk down. Sean crumpled fast. The guy couldn't take any kind of blow.

"Davis!" Jamie yelled. "Don't!" Then she grabbed his arm again. "I can handle this."

But he didn't want Sean hurting her. Every word Sean said…it *hurt*. Did Jamie think he couldn't tell? He could. He felt her pain all around him.

Jamie released him. She put her hands on her hips and glared down at Sean. "How much?"

Sean pushed up to his feet. His angry stare flickered to Davis. "You got cop friends down here, too? Will they save you when I press charges?"

Davis shrugged. "Let's find out."

Jamie put herself between them. "You shouldn't be here, Sean. Go back home. You've done enough damage."

And, just like that, the guy seemed to wilt. His head sagged, and his eyes closed. "Fifty thousand. He paid me fifty thousand dollars, okay? To tell him what I knew, then to keep quiet about it. I wasn't ever supposed to tell anyone. Fifty thousand…it can buy a whole lot of silence."

"Only you didn't stay silent," Davis said. Anger turned his words into a growl.

"No." Sean's gaze slid toward Jamie. There

was emotion in his stare. Regret. Longing. Sean jerked his thumb toward Davis. "When he told me what was happening to you, I couldn't keep quiet. Hurting you was never part of the deal."

You should have never made any deal.

"It's been so long," Sean continued, his voice roughening. "I thought he had to be different by now. I mean...so much time has passed. He's got a job. Garrison said he'd finished his therapy years ago. Henry was supposed to be a changed man."

"Some people can't change," Jamie said. Her gaze was on Sean.

She means you, idiot. You didn't change. You sold her out this time just like you did before.

"I want to make this right," Sean said, sounding desperate. "Please, tell me what to do. How can I make this right?"

Davis gazed at Jamie. She was staring at Sean as if she were looking at a stranger. Maybe to her, the guy truly was a stranger. She'd thought he was someone else, long ago; then she'd learned the truth.

Just like Ava and my brothers...we're all slowly learning the truth about what happened to our parents. What we've believed for so long is wrong. There are so many secrets.

Secrets and lies. Long forgotten sins. They were everywhere.

"Jamie, please," Sean said, his voice sharpening. "Talk to me. We were friends, lovers. You have to know I wouldn't put you in danger!"

But Jamie's laughter was so bitter. So cold. Not at all like the woman Davis knew. "Being my lover doesn't matter. It sure didn't matter to Henry." She shook her head. "There's nothing you can do." Then she was looking away from him, her gaze focusing on the shell of her house once again.

"You should leave," Sean told her, edging closer to her. "I brought… I brought twenty grand with me. It's yours, Jamie. Take it and run. Start over again. I won't tell this time, I won't tell anyone—"

"I'm not going to run any longer."

Davis stiffened.

"I want to have a life here."

With me?

"I don't want to keep looking over my shoulder. I want to stop Henry—stop him for good because I've already lost enough of my life to him. I've lost enough," she said, her voice determined, her delicate jaw hardening. "And I'm not going to be afraid any longer. I ran, I hid and I lost everything. But he's the one who should have suffered." Her hands had clenched into fists. Tears filled her eyes, but Davis could tell—those tears were from anger. "He's the one who should have been punished. He's the one who should have lost everything." Each word carried her rage, a rage that she deserved to feel. She'd held her pain and fury inside for too long. It was time to let it go.

"I won't lose anything else," Jamie vowed. "*He* will. If he is doing this to me, then I'll prove it."

We will, Davis thought. Because he was going to be at her side the whole time.

"And there won't be any more hiding behind his father. He'll pay for what he's done." Jamie exhaled and said again, her voice determined, "I won't lose."

SULLIVAN DID A double take as he stared into that room. The man staring back at him, with wide, startled eyes…he had Henry Westport's brown hair. He had Henry's bright blue eyes.

Same build. Same height.

"Get the hell out of here," the guard barked as he shoved at Sullivan. "Go!" Then he turned toward the patient. "We have to get out of here, Henry. The alarm is sounding."

"Henry" nodded. But Sullivan just blocked the doorway. "You're not Henry Westport." It was the jaw. This guy's jaw was harder than Henry's. And his brows…they were shaped differently. His nose was a little too long. Small differences, but they added up. Sullivan had studied Henry's picture, he *knew* what the guy looked like.

This man is close, but he's not Henry Westport.

"Of course I'm Henry," the man snapped, and he tried to glare at Sullivan, but the fear in the fellow's eyes made that glare worthless. "And there's a fire, we have to leave—"

"There's no fire, and you're not Henry." Hell, a double. Someone had hired a double to take Henry's place. How long had this been going on? Had Garrison hired the guy when his son vanished? Or *so* his son could vanish? Or maybe Henry had even cooked up this scheme himself.

"I'm Henry Westport," the guy snapped again, and he even had a clipped New England accent edging the words. A nice touch, but total baloney. "Look, you need to get out of here. You need—"

The guard charged at Sullivan. All three hundred bulky pounds of him. Sullivan sighed, sidestepped, then grabbed for the fellow. He let the guard's own momentum work against him, and soon he was crashing into the wall, hitting hard enough to stun, then slumping toward the floor.

Sullivan smiled at "Henry."

"So…how about we try this again? Who the hell are you? And where's the real Henry Westport?"

The man stepped back. His gaze swept the room, as if seeking an escape. There wasn't one.

Sullivan closed in on him. "We can do this the easy way…you just tell me what I want to know…" He rolled his neck, loosened his muscles and said, "Or in five minutes, I'll have you *begging* to tell me—"

"I've been here a little over a month!" the guy squeaked. That fancy accent was gone. "They paid me…hell, it's like a free vacation. I've done it before, whenever the guy needs to slip away. Easy cash." He put his hands up in front of him. "It's just like an acting gig!"

No, it wasn't.

"I'm an actor!" the fellow said, voice frantic. "This helps to cushion me, you know, between jobs. So what if a rich and famous guy wants to slip away—doesn't hurt anyone, right?"

Wrong. Dead Wrong.

"Where is the real Henry Westport?"

The actor licked his lips. "I have no idea."

Chapter Ten

The new lover was in his way. An annoyance that would have to be eliminated. But some research had shown him that it wasn't just one McGuire that he had to worry about. It was the whole damn family.

Private investigators. Ex-military. Not such easy prey. He'd have to be careful with them. Maybe…perhaps it would be easier to work around them.

He watched as the vehicles drove away. They'd all been right there, staring at the torched remains of the house. Jamie had even walked toward him at one point. Had she sensed that he was close? He'd been staring straight at her, not daring to move at all. She'd inched closer. Closer.

The wind had lifted her hair. Tossed it against her cheeks. She was blonder now. Her hair streaked with gold. From all the time in that Texas sun? And her body was curvier.

But her eyes were still the same. So big, so innocent. So—

Lying.

She had plans of her own. He'd heard her. She thought to get some payback? Anger had whipped within him at those words, and it had taken all of his self-control to stay still. But lunging out and attacking then—no, that wouldn't have been smart.

Three against one. Those odds weren't to his advantage.

Better to attack…one on one.

Better to take Jamie away. To lure her to me.

And he knew exactly how to make that happen.

Sean Nyle had proven to be so useful over the years. He'd hated the man, of course; he was sleaze, but a useful sleaze. It was time for the man to be of use again.

So he waited, waited until the vehicles were completely gone, then he finally moved. His muscles were stiff, and pinpricks shot through his feet as feeling came back to his toes. How long had he been still? He wasn't sure.

He'd just come out there on a whim, wanting to be close to Jamie. Then she'd appeared.

We'll always be linked.

He hoped she understood that. She needed

to see that no other would ever understand her the way he did. What they shared—no one could touch it.

And they'd better not try.

He started his motorcycle, revving it up. He knew a short cut that would take him to the main road. He might even beat the other cars there. It was a good thing he'd taken his time learning this area. It made it so much easier to hunt his prey.

I'll start with you, Sean...because you aren't getting in my way.

It was better to begin with the simplest prey.

DAVIS STOPPED HIS vehicle in the lot of Jamie's clinic. They hadn't spoken during the ride over. Jamie had been staring out of the window, seemingly a million miles away from him.

He wanted her back with him. In the here and now. He didn't want to lose her to ghosts.

"I meant what I said." Jamie turned to stare at him. "I'm not going to run. And the other night...it was fear driving me. Fear telling me to go, but I'm tired of being afraid."

I never want her afraid again.

She smiled at him, and that slow smile—it nearly broke his heart.

When did I get a heart that could break?

"Thank you," she told him.

He shook his head. "Sweetheart, you don't need to thank me for anything."

"I do. Thank you…for laughing at the wedding."

Now she'd made him frown. He didn't remember—

"I heard you laugh." Her smile stretched a bit. "When I did my best to knock that bouquet away from me. And then I turned around and you were there. You'd been there before, I'd seen you over the past year. But that time…that time I thought…" Jamie exhaled. "*He's here now.* Like you'd been waiting for me."

Waiting for her to turn and see him there. *I had been.*

"You've helped me over the past few days, more than I can ever say." Her smile turned a bit pained, rueful. "And I've repaid you with danger, and I know that's not a fair exchange. I know—"

He leaned forward and kissed her. A hard brush of his lips over hers. One that made him want to do far more. "You don't have to thank me. Not for anything." Because he wanted to be with her. Wanting to protect her was second nature to him. He needed Jamie safe. Needed all threats to her to be eliminated.

And that's why I'm about to go and pay a little visit to Sean Nyle. They would have a serious chat. *I told him to stay away. He didn't listen.*

Davis hadn't wanted to attack the guy, not with Jamie watching. Not with her trying to get him to hold back.

But in a few moments, Jamie wouldn't be there.

"Mac is already waiting inside for you," he said.

"My guard, for the day?" Jamie shook her head. "He doesn't have to do that. He—"

"For me, okay? Keep him close because I want to make sure nothing happens to you."

"Nothing will."

It had damn well better not.

Then she kissed him. She leaned in and brushed her lips over his cheek. "I always knew you were one of the good guys." She turned before he could say anything else and hopped from the vehicle. She hurried into the clinic, stopping just long enough to toss him a quick wave over her shoulder.

One of the good guys.

She had that wrong. Just because he wasn't evil, well, that didn't mean he was good.

Davis waited until she went inside, then he reversed his vehicle. He hit the Bluetooth connection and called Grant.

"Sean Nyle is in town," he said.

"What? The ex?"

Yeah, a guy who needed to realize he was an *ex* for a reason. Davis hadn't liked the way that the other man had stared at Jamie. *As if he still wants her.*

That wasn't happening. Sean would never have her again. He'd hurt her before, and Davis didn't want him close to Jamie ever again.

I warned him. He should have listened.

"He drove into town. The guy was just out at Jamie's house." What was left of it. "I need to know where he is. It's early, so I figure he stayed at a motel around here last night."

"I'll do some checking," Grant said immediately. "I'll call you when I find him."

And in the meantime, Davis would start heading toward the closest motel to Jamie's property. If he'd been Sean, if he'd wanted to see Jamie…*then I would have booked the place closest to her.*

Following that hunch, Davis pushed the gas pedal down on the floor and took off.

"Jamie?"

She looked up. Sylvia stood behind her

desk. And Mac—he was sitting in the corner chair of the lobby, seemingly engrossed in a magazine—but looking totally out of place, like a big, dangerous jungle cat who'd wandered in by mistake.

"What's happening?" Sylvia asked. "And don't tell me nothing." She pointed toward Mac. "You've had a bodyguard, for two days straight." Sylvia's eyes reflected her worry. "I think I deserve to know what's going on, I think—"

"You do."

From the corner of her eye, she saw Mac put down his magazine.

"You deserve to know everything, and I'm not going to hide it anymore." She'd carried this secret around for so long, like a dark sin that she wanted to keep from the rest of the world. *I didn't do anything wrong.* "There's something you need to know about me."

Sylvia hurried around the desk. She took Jamie's hand. "What is it?"

A long and twisted tale. "Let's go into my office," Jamie told her. "And I'll tell you all about the girl I used to be."

Because if Sylvia was going to stay with her, she needed to know about the danger closing in.

JAMIE HATED HIM.

Sean slammed his car door shut and hurried toward the motel room. The guilt had been eating him alive ever since Davis McGuire appeared at his office. Sean had gone to Jamie, thinking he could maybe try and make things right.

Then he'd seen her house. The place had been torched straight to the ground. And Jamie—she'd had fear in her eyes when she first saw him.

She used to smile when their eyes met. She'd glow a bit. They'd laugh. Share secrets.

But they'd lost all of that.

We didn't lose it. I killed it.

Because he'd been on the verge of having his dreams slip away. His family had hit a rough spot, and even the student loans wouldn't have been enough to finance his education. His dreams, he'd always had plenty of them.

So he'd told a few lies. At the time, he'd even convinced himself...*what would it hurt?*

But then, he'd seen the way the others at school had turned on Jamie. Guilt had eaten at him, gnawing away more and more each day and then—

Jamie had just been gone. She'd vanished.

The guilt had eased. He'd gone on with his life. He'd screwed up again. Why did he always seem to hurt the people closest to him?

And he'd gone back to square one. No money. Few prospects and...

Jamie.

At the wrong time, in the right place.

He hurried toward his motel room door. Fumbling a bit with the key, he managed to get the door open. He rushed inside, jerking a hand through his hair.

Garrison had told him that he just wanted to make sure Jamie was safe. Maybe...maybe Garrison didn't know what his son was doing. Maybe he could call the guy and get him down there. Maybe Jamie could be safe again, and this whole mess could vanish.

And the gnawing guilt will leave me once more.

Maybe. He yanked out his phone. Called the number Garrison had left for him, a number he'd programmed in his phone, just in case. The line rang, once. Twice.

"Come on, come on..." Sean muttered.

And the line was picked up. "Why are you calling me?" Garrison demanded.

Sean blinked. Oh, right, caller ID. "Because we've got a situation." He paced around the cramped confines of that motel room. "Have you ever heard of McGuire Securities? Because if you haven't, you sure need to know about them."

"I'm aware of the situation." Garrison's voice sounded annoyed.

Annoyed? The guy needed to be scared. "Are you *aware* that Jamie's house was torched? That the only thing left is some sagging walls that have been charred pitch-black? Are you aware of that?"

Silence.

"I'm close to her," Sean said. "I had to come and see for myself. She's being stalked, and I thought you were going to keep her safe." His fingers clenched around the phone. "That was what you told me, right? That you were worried about—"

"It's not her safety that concerns me," Garrison said, his voice curt. "And that's not what should concern you, either."

"What?"

"You need to look after yourself." Now Garrison's voice hardened even more. "Do you understand me, Nyle? Watch yourself. You shouldn't have gone to find her. You said you weren't having any contact with her. That made you safe. But if you've gone back to her, with the past you two share—"

A knock sounded at Sean's door. He turned, frowning. Was that the maid? He should have hung up one of those do-not-disturb signs, but he'd been a little distracted. *Freaking understatement.*

"Where's your son?" he asked Garrison as he headed toward the door. "Because I'm thinking he's down here. I'm thinking—" He yanked open the door.

And a knife shoved into his stomach.

Sean gasped, and the phone slipped from his hand.

"NYLE?" GARRISON WESTPORT demanded as he leaned forward. His driver was nearly at the airport. "Nyle, dammit, don't you leave me hanging—"

He heard a strangled gasp. A thud.

Then…laughter?

"Nyle?" Garrison repeated.

But there was no response. He sat back, slumping a bit against the leather seat. This was all out of control. Everything…it shouldn't be happening. He'd worked so hard, for so long.

It shouldn't be happening.

"Drive faster," he said. Because he was afraid that the present was about to become even bloodier than the past.

And he was too far away to stop it.

Helpless, just like he'd been before.

SYLVIA STARED AT JAMIE.

Just stared at her.

"So, um…that's it." She'd talked fast, barely taking a breath as she revealed all the dark skeletons that hung in her closet. Only those skeletons weren't hiding any longer. They were out, for all the world to see.

Henry's already found me. There's no point in hiding.

"It?" Sylvia repeated. She rose and shook her head.

Jamie tensed.

"That's not 'it'!" Sylvia said. "That's a nightmare. That's hell. That's—" She broke off and hugged Jamie, hard. "That's what you've been holding back. You think I couldn't see it? Pain has always clung to you, and I hated it." Sylvia sniffed. "I'm sorry."

Jamie caught her friend's arms. "Why?"

"I'm sorry you've carried this for so long, all alone." Sylvia gave her a small smile. "But you're not alone anymore, right?"

Sylvia believes me.

"Right," Jamie said, her voice soft. "I'm not alone anymore."

Perhaps she never had been. Her own fear

had stopped her from seeing what was right in front of her all along. Friends. Support.

Jamie thought of Davis.

Maybe even love.

WHEN HE PULLED into the motel's parking lot, Davis saw Sean's blue SUV. Davis parked his rental right next to it, then glanced over at the motel.

Sean's vehicle was parked directly in front of room number seven. Eyes narrowing, Davis climbed from his car. He hurried toward the door. His fist lifted, and he pounded against the old wood. "Sean Nyle!"

He heard a thud from inside. The fast pad of footsteps.

He took a step back from that door. "Open up, Sean! We need to talk!" No other cars were in the lot. All of the other guests must have cleared out early.

He glanced back at the lot. Wait…

There *was* another vehicle there. Over near the dumpster, half-hidden, he could just make out a motorcycle.

A motor—*hell*.

He swung back toward the door. "Sean!" He looked down. Saw faint red splotches on the cement. Red drops of…blood?

He grabbed for the knob. The door was unlocked, so he shoved it open and rushed inside.

Davis saw Sean, slumped near the bed, huddled in a pool of growing blood. Swearing, Davis ran for him.

Sean tried to turn toward Davis. The guy's eyes were bleary. "No...behind...door—"

Dammit! Rookie mistake. Rookie—

Before Davis could turn back around, something heavy slammed into his head. Davis fell down, and darkness swam before him.

JAMIE'S PHONE RANG. Frowning, she pulled it from the pocket of her scrubs. She saw Davis's number on the screen and glanced apologetically at Sylvia. "I need to take this, I—"

"I understand," Sylvia told her. Sylvia's gaze was filled with sympathy and worry. "I'll be outside."

Jamie nodded. Her finger was poised to swipe over the screen and take Davis's call.

Sylvia hesitated at the door. "I'm glad you told me, Jamie."

"Me, too." She was. Glad one more person knew her secrets.

She'd guarded those secrets, as if they were dark, painful sins for so long. *But they weren't my sins.*

And she was tired of paying for them.

Her finger swiped over the screen, and she lifted the phone to her ear. "Davis, what's—"

"I missed you."

She knew that voice, knew it at once. Goose bumps rose on her arms, and Jamie felt all the blood drain from her face.

"You didn't miss me, though, did you? You just found someone else. Moved on, as if I didn't matter."

"Henry." She should move. Run into the hallway. Get Mac. Let him know that Henry was on the line. *I knew Henry was down here. No one else would want to burn my house. No one else would want to—*

"One is dead, and one is still alive. But there sure is a lot of blood."

Her heart stopped. "Wh-what?"

"Your lovers," he said, as if she should understand. "I'm looking at them now. One is dead, and one is still alive."

He called me on Davis's phone! Nausea rose in her throat even as she stumbled toward the door.

"I don't really care about them." His voice was so mild, as if he were just talking about the weather. Not life or death. "It's you that matters. You've always mattered to me."

"Then leave them alone!" *One is dead.* Not Davis. Not Davis, *please.*

"Come to me, and I will. I'll leave them just as they are. Maybe help will arrive. Maybe one will live. But I need you to come to me, Jamie."

"I will," she promised. She would have promised anything if it meant that Davis would be all right. "Where are you?"

"At your house, Jamie...well, what's left of it." His voice snapped then. "I had to punish you for all those long years. Years that we should have spent together."

He's not any better. The stories were wrong. He's just as twisted as he was before.

No, he was worse.

"Go back to your house, Jamie. Come back alone. Just you and me, and I'll leave them where they are."

"Where are they?" Jamie whispered.

"The motel. Sean's motel room. Both of them are there." Static crackled over the line. "Tell me, which one do you want to live? The one who sold you out? Or the one who was coming to fight for you? Davis McGuire... he's a lot like me, Jamie."

"He's nothing like you."

"He's got that killer instinct. I know what

he was coming here to do. I just beat him to the punch."

Jamie shook her head. "He's *nothing* like you," she said again.

He just laughed. "You're coming to me, aren't you, Jamie?"

"Yes."

"See you soon, sweet Jamie. So soon…"

He hung up on her, and she raced into the hallway. "Mac!"

Chapter Eleven

At her cry, Mac shot up from his seat and lunged toward her.

Jamie's whole body was shaking.

"What's happening?" Mac demanded. He grabbed her arms, holding tight.

And she clung to him just as fiercely. "You have to get to Davis. He's hurt." *Not dead. Not dead. Not Davis.*

"What?"

"Henry just called me." Her words were tumbling out, and she didn't even know if they were making sense. "He said…he said he was at Sean's motel room. That Davis and Sean—they were there, hurt." Her breath burned in her lungs, but the rest of her body felt ice cold. "He told me one of them was dead."

Mac paled.

And then she heard a ringing. Not her phone this time, but his. Mac pulled away and yanked the phone out. He looked at the screen, then put the phone to his ear. "Grant, we've got a problem. It's Davis—" He broke off, listened for a moment, then said, "We need the cops there. Jamie just said that freak Henry called her—"

"From Davis's phone," she whispered.

Mac tensed. "She said he's hurt Davis. Hell, yes, I'm on my way there now. No, no, he damn well better be all right." He shoved the phone back down. His eyes shone with fury and deadly intent. "Grant told me the motel's location. He's en route and so am I. We'll get the cops there—"

"But—"

"You stay here. With that guy running around loose, who the hell knows what he'll do next?"

I know. He told me where he was going. "But, Mac, he said—"

She was talking to air. Mac had already run out of the door.

"Ohmygod…" That stunned whisper came from behind Jamie. She whirled around. Sylvia was there, staring at her with wide, stark eyes. "The man you told me about… Henry… he's really here?"

"Not here," Jamie said. She was still ice cold. Numb. *Davis has to be all right.* "He's on his way to my house—my property. I need to get the cops out there." And she needed to get to Davis's side. "Can I borrow your car?" Jamie asked because she could already hear the growl of Mac's engine outside. She had to hurry if she was going to follow him, and her car was out at the McGuire ranch.

Sylvia nodded, her eyes wide and scared as she tossed Jamie the keys.

Jamie caught them in midair. "Thank you," she called out as she raced for the door. There were no clients around—thank goodness—but if they had been there, she still would have run right through them. *Davis.* He was all she could think about. She had to get to him.

Mac was dead wrong if he thought Jamie would sit in the background while Davis needed her.

She rushed toward Sylvia's car, shoved the key into the lock—

And saw the man's reflection in the window. Big, broad shoulders, wearing a ski mask—

Jamie spun around and opened her mouth to scream, but he slapped his hand over her lips.

"Missed you..."

This time, she could see his eyes. That cold blue stare that she'd never been able to forget.

"I knew you'd call the cops on me…I know you so well…I just needed you to come outside…" And he lifted his hand. His fingers curled around the syringe he had there. "Borrowed this from your office last night."

She kicked out at him, aiming for his groin.

"If it can knock out a horse, it should work on you."

She kicked harder. His hold slipped, and she managed to surge away from him. "Sylvia!" Jamie screamed. *"Help—"*

He grabbed her and jammed the needle into her neck. The pain was fast, white-hot, pouring through her veins. She kept fighting him, but her movements quickly grew sluggish. Her body started to sag, and he looped his arms around her waist, hauling her back toward the other car there. A vehicle she hadn't even noticed moments before. A car that was…

Davis's? Yes, it was the SUV he'd rented after his truck had been totaled, and she clawed at the door, holding it tightly because Jamie was afraid that if he drove away with her…

She'd never escape him again.

She tried to scream, but only a rough whisper escaped from her.

"Get in the damn car!" Henry snarled at her, and he hit her, a blow that sent her slumping back.

"Jamie!"

She managed to turn her head. Henry had slammed the door, and he was running toward the driver's side. But that cry—that had been Sylvia's cry. Sylvia was racing out of the clinic and toward them.

Jamie just had to open the car door. She had to get to her friend.

But her fingers weren't working properly. Actually, she couldn't feel them at all. She could only sag against the window, staring helplessly, as Henry raced away. Her gaze was on Sylvia. She could see her friend screaming.

And Jamie could do nothing.

"Davis!"

He heard the roar as if it came from a distance, but the hard hands shaking him—they were sure up close and personal. A rough grip tightened around his shoulders, and the shaking started again. "Dammit, Davis, you look at me, now!"

Footsteps. Pounding. "Stop it, Mac!" Another rough shout. "He's got a head wound, he needs—"

"Jamie." The one word sounded like a

croak from him, but just saying her name
gave Davis strength. He forced his eyes open,
and he saw Mac crouching above him. Mac
was the one who'd been shaking him. The
one staring down at him in horror.

Just how bad do I look?

"I thought you were gone," Mac muttered,
and his brother was as pale as a ghost. "Dammit, don't ever do that crap to me again."

He could hear the distant scream of a siren.
Davis tried to sit up, but his head pounded
so hard that nausea rolled through his whole
body. "He...hit me..."

"Uh, from the look of things..." Grant was
there, too, standing just a few feet away. He
pointed to the floor. "The guy broke a chair
over your head."

He'd gone into the room, seen Sean and—

He whipped around, and, for a moment,
the pounding in his head grew so strong that
the whole room darkened. *No, not again.* But
then the darkness lightened to gray, and he
could see Sean. Only, Sean wasn't moving.

"There wasn't anything I could do for
him," Mac said, voice gruff. "He was gone
by the time I got here."

*But he was still alive when I came in. If
I hadn't let that SOB get the drop on me, I
could have helped him. I could have—*

"It was Henry," Mac said as the sirens grew louder. "He called Jamie. Told her that you were here. Man, I haven't been that scared since—" His lips clamped shut and he just said, "Never do that again."

He called Jamie. Those words echoed through his pounding head as Davis tried to push himself up. Tried, failed, twice, but Mac helped him, and he finally staggered to his feet. "Where is she?"

"She's safe," Mac said, his hands moving to steady Davis. "She's at the clinic with Sylvia. Don't worry."

But he was worried because… Henry was here. Henry was obsessed with Jamie. Henry had just *killed* Sean—

Why didn't he kill me?

The guy had the opportunity. Davis had been helpless once he hit the floor. *So why am I still alive?*

"Need…her," Davis said. He hated that his words sounded so slurred. Hated that black spots kept dancing before his eyes.

"Yeah, yeah, I get that," Mac assured him.

Grant came around and slid his shoulders under Davis's arm.

The room smelled of blood. Of death.

I need Jamie.

"Let's get you patched up," Grant said.

Worry roughened his voice. "And we'll get Jamie to meet us at the hospital."

"I don't want...to go...hospital..." Davis muttered. "Want—"

"Jamie, yes, we've got that, but you have to get checked out. The guy split open your head," Mac said, voice still gruff. "And you looked dead when I burst into that room. Do you hear me? *Dead.* You're going to get stitched up, then we'll find that creep—"

"Find... Jamie...get her..." He had to see her, had to touch her. *Need her.*

"We'll get her," Grant promised.

"I'll bring her to the hospital, okay?" Mac said quickly. "Just calm down. I get that she's important, I get it."

They were outside. He could see the bright swirl of lights. An ambulance was there, and Davis was slowly lowered onto a stretcher.

"I'll bring her," Mac promised him. "You just don't do anything dumb, like dying on me, got it?"

The bright lights made his head ache even worse. "Got...it."

THE STREET SPOKE of money and prestige. The perfect houses, the well-manicured lawns. Everything was in perfect place.

Sullivan stared up at 5320 Wind Crest. The

home that belonged to Jamie's parents, parents that she hadn't seen in years.

Sullivan had gone to that address because something about the case was nagging at him.

Like it's just one thing.

He should have been preparing to fly back home. At the very least, he needed to call and check in with Davis but...

A piece of the puzzle is missing.

Because he'd actually believed Garrison when the man said he'd been getting notes. Letters about the past. Only Sullivan didn't think Jamie had been sending those notes.

He headed toward the door. There were no guards at this house. No security cameras. He pressed the bell and heard the happy barking of a dog. He tensed at the sound, and a few moments later, the door opened.

The small, white dog was held in a woman's arm. A woman with blond hair and blue eyes. A woman who looked far more like Jamie's sister than she did her mother. Her face was perfectly made up, her makeup absolutely flawless. Her skin was creamy, clear, and he didn't see even a single line on her face.

She frowned at him, only the frown moved just part of her face. "May I help you?"

"Penelope? Penelope Bridgeton?"

"Yes." But she backed up a step and suddenly appeared wary. "Who are you? What do you want?"

This was a gamble. A big one. "I'm a friend of your daughter's."

Her lips trembled. Her eyes seemed to tear up. "That's not funny. How dare you come to me and—" She drew herself up.

The dog growled at Sullivan.

"Get off my property," she said. "Don't ever come back or I will call the police." She started to close the door in his face.

He caught the edge of the door. The dog growled again. "She looks like you," Sullivan told her bluntly. "A lot like you."

Penelope's mascara wasn't quite so perfect anymore.

"Do you miss her?" She had to miss her daughter, didn't she? Miss her enough to potentially do something reckless? "Do you think about what happened when you sit in this big house? A house that her pain probably bought for you?"

"Get out..." Then her voice rose. "Ray! Raymond, get in here! Help me!"

More footsteps, rushing in the direction of the door. Sullivan looked to the right and saw a tall, dark-haired man coming toward him. While Penelope had aged well—or with help—the man appeared haggard. Too thin.

Old before his time. His hair was shot through with silver.

"Get away from my wife!" Raymond Bridgeton blasted.

Sullivan dropped his hand and freed the door. "My mistake. I thought you two might care about what's happening with Jamie." He shook his head. "After all, I'm pretty sure it was *your* letters that set Henry off, Mrs. Bridgeton."

She paled. "Wh-what's happening?"

But Raymond pushed her back into the foyer. "Call the police. This man—he's lying to you. He doesn't know our Jamie. He—"

"She's a veterinarian, do you know that? Finished her studies, and she's been practicing for years. She's got a dog named Jinx, a real wild one that only listens to her." He inclined his head. "And I think she was happy... until someone torched her house. Until she was run off the road. But, hey, what do you care, right? You haven't seen her in years. Not your problem anymore, I get that. Like I said, my mistake." He turned on his heel.

Sullivan had taken two steps when a hand grabbed his arm and yanked him back around. He stared into Penelope's tear-filled eyes. "Is Jamie okay?"

Sympathy moved in him. "She was when

I left her. My brother's looking after her. He cares about her." Sullivan suspected that Davis's feelings were a whole lot more complex than just caring, but he stuck with that safe word.

"I miss her," Penelope whispered. "And I am so sorry." Her tears came then—hard, wrenching tears that shook her entire body and splotched her face. "I'm so sorry." She crumpled, and she would have fallen to her knees, but Raymond grabbed her. He held her tight. Grief and pain were clear on his face, too.

Raymond blinked his eyes a few times, his Adam's apple bobbed, and he rasped, "You really know our Jamie?"

"Yes, I—" His phone rang. And the ringtone told him that it was his brother Grant. "Excuse me," he murmured. Bad timing. He answered the phone. "Look, Grant, I'll call you right back—"

"I'm on the way to the hospital with Davis."

His breath rushed out.

"He was attacked, and Mac is saying that Henry called Jamie, that the guy confessed to her—"

"It *is* Henry," Sullivan said even as his heart began to race fast in his chest. "The guy has a double that he's been using up here, a guy who pretends to be him in the psych facility. From what I can tell, the real Henry Westport has been gone for at least a month." *And has he been stalking Jamie in Texas that whole time?* "Is Davis all right?" His hold on the phone was far too tight.

"He's going to be fine." Grant sounded determined. "But Sean Nyle wasn't so lucky. Henry stabbed him five times—once in the heart, a wound that guy couldn't survive."

Hell. "Tell me that he's in custody."

"Not yet. We need you back here, man. *Now.*"

"I'm on the way." It was happening again. His family needed him—and he was too far away to do any good. His worst nightmare. When his parents had been attacked, he'd been an ocean away on a Black Ops mission. It had taken days for the news to reach him. He hadn't even gotten home in time for the funeral.

He glanced back at Jamie's parents. She hadn't talked to them in years. They were alive, a phone call away from her, but she'd turned her back on them.

Because they sold her out. "How much was your daughter worth?" He looked at the fancy house. "And are you coming to realize that whatever they gave you, it could never be enough?" He would give anything, pay any price, if he could have his parents back with him.

"We made a mistake," Penelope said, voice and face tormented. "Jamie was alive, safe... We thought they'd keep Henry locked up. Garrison told us that he'd never been like that before, that he would never be a threat to her again."

Get to Davis.

"Your son didn't believe that, did he? That's why he was with Jamie. He was protecting her."

A tear slid down her cheek, taking a black trail of mascara with it. "We protected Jamie, too..."

His eyes narrowed.

Raymond put his hands around Penelope's thin shoulders. "How do you think the US Marshals got involved? Once we saw that the Westports were never going to leave her alone—"

"Even bribing that terrible Sean Nyle to lie about her," Penelope gritted.

The way you lied, too?

"I called in every favor I had," Raymond

continued. "And, yeah, some of those strings involved Garrison."

Garrison had been in on the US Marshal deal?

"I would have made a deal with the devil then if I thought it would keep Jamie safe."

He *had* dealt with the devil.

"Garrison pulled strings. We got Jamie that new life. We got Jamie away from all the pain and fear."

No, sir, you didn't. She's been afraid this whole time.

"She didn't know it," Raymond continued gruffly, "but I helped to get her set up in a new place, with a new life. It broke my heart, but I knew it had to be done. She was losing more and more of herself every day. She had to get away." He swallowed. "From us all."

And I have to go, too. "My brother's in the hospital," Sullivan told them. "I have to go back to him."

Penelope stepped forward. "But Jamie… she's okay? She's…happy?"

He nodded and turned to leave.

"If she…if she ever asks about us, will you tell her how sorry I am? Every day that passes, every year…" Her voice dropped. "I miss her more and more."

Sullivan glanced back at her. "Is that why

you sent those notes to Garrison and Henry? Because you miss Jamie—"

Her eyes glinted. "I miss her, and I hate them."

And he knew with one hundred percent certainty that she'd sent the notes. Notes that had stirred up a man's obsession. Or, hell, maybe that obsession had been there all along, and Henry had just finally gotten lucky and found Jamie again.

Because if Davis was in the hospital, if he'd been taken out, then Sullivan knew exactly who Henry's next target would be…

Jamie.

JAMIE'S EYES SLOWLY OPENED. It was dark around her, so dark, but she could hear a faint…grinding sound.

She reached out and realized that her hands were tied. A thick, rough rope circled her wrists. She stretched her legs and found that her ankles were bound, too.

How long was I out?

She kept stretching, lifting her bound hands and feet as she tried to figure out—

She hit something. Something hard. Something metal? She pushed, moving her hands, and realized that she was in a very, very small space.

The grinding quieted and then…stopped. Jamie rolled.

Rolled.

And she realized where she was. The dark space. Too tight. The sound that she could hear—it was tires, on a road. Henry had tied her up and tossed her in a trunk. Maybe he'd even switched vehicles so that no one would be able to find them. After all, the police would look for Davis's rental, so he'd probably ditched it and stolen another ride. And now he had her in the trunk—

The grinding increased again as he sped up. He had her in the trunk, and he was taking her away. When the car stopped, Jamie knew exactly what would happen.

He'll kill me. Maybe not right away, but she knew his endgame. She'd run away from him. He'd told her before that she couldn't betray him.

But she *had* betrayed him. On every level. She'd slipped away from him. She'd made a new life. She'd found someone to love.

Tears stung her eyes. She *did* love Davis. She'd never told him. Neither of them had spoken about their feelings. Yet as she lay trapped in that darkness, Jamie knew the truth.

It was nice to know that truth. Nice to

know that, before she died, she'd gotten the chance to see what love was really like.

It wasn't twisted. Wasn't obsessed. It was strong. It was sensual. It made you feel happy when you were with the other person...and, love—love pushed the fear away.

The vehicle began to slow again. Jamie's body rolled a bit, but she braced her legs.

Then...silence. He'd turned off the car's engine.

Her bound hands flew around the trunk, looking for some kind of weapon. Something that she could use. Because she didn't want to die.

Love did something else, too.

It made her want to live. Made her want to see Davis, just one more time.

A million more times.

But there was nothing in the back for her to use. No jack. No crowbar. Just her.

A car door slammed. She could hear the thud of footsteps. He was coming for her.

Jamie twisted her body. Maybe he didn't realize that she was awake. Maybe he thought the drug would keep her knocked out or weak. Only she didn't feel weak.

She heard a faint squeak, and then the trunk's lid began to open.

"Oh, Jamie..." Henry murmured, and his voice was from her nightmares. "I've missed you so."

The truck's lid lifted, lifted—

Jamie could see Henry. The ski mask was gone, and he was smiling down at her as the sun hit his brown hair. His bright blue eyes seemed to be lit with madness. He reached out to her.

Jamie drove her feet into his stomach. She hit him as hard as she could, and he stumbled back. Jamie flopped out of the trunk, hauling herself up and then plummeting face-first onto the ground. She wiggled until she got on her feet, and she tried to jump her way to freedom. She'd get to—

His laughter filled the air.

"God, I've missed you."

Then he slammed his hand into her back and Jamie hit the ground once again. She rolled over and found a knife pressed to her throat.

He smiled down at her. Henry. The boy she'd thought she loved, a lifetime ago. Still handsome.

Still insane.

"Just like old times, isn't it?" He moved the knife down to her side. "Old...times..."

Jamie screamed.

POLICE CARS WERE at Jamie's clinic.

Mac braked, then jumped out of his vehicle. Oh, hell, no. This couldn't be good. He ran forward and saw Sylvia. She was crying as she talked with two uniformed cops. Where was Jamie? Inside?

"Sylvia!"

Her head whipped up at his shout. When she saw him, she seemed to cry harder.

"Sylvia, where's Jamie? Davis needs her!"

She shook her head, and the cops turned toward him.

His gut clenched. "What happened?" *I left, running blindly to get to Davis. But he'd told me to stay with Jamie. To protect her.*

Mac advanced slowly now, not wanting to hear what Sylvia was about to say because he knew, he *knew* Davis would never forgive him.

My brother loves her. I know it, even if he hasn't realized it yet. He'd seen it, in the way Davis looked at Jamie. In the way he talked about her.

"A—a man in a ski mask took her," Sylvia said.

Mac felt his world stop.

"I was screaming for her, running to help, but he drove away." Sylvia's hands clenched in front of her. "He put a needle in her neck—

I saw him—and he just…" Her voice became hushed. "He drove away with Jamie."

Davis would go insane.

My fault.

"We have an APB out for the vehicle," one of the cops told him. "The driver is unknown so—"

No, he wasn't unknown. "The driver is a man named Henry Westport, and if we don't find him and Jamie soon, he will kill her."

Chapter Twelve

"I'm leaving," Davis said as he glared at his doctor. Yes, his head still hurt like hell, but they'd stitched him up. He didn't intend to stay in some hospital bed for the next twenty-four hours while the doctors and nurses poked and prodded him. He wanted to be out there, hunting Henry Westport.

"Sir," the doctor—a woman with warm caramel skin and dark, intense eyes—shook her head. "I don't think you understand the seriousness of your situation. You've sustained a traumatic brain injury. Concussions aren't just simple matters to shrug off."

"Yeah, well…" He swung his legs over the side of the bed and made sure to show no signs of the dizziness he felt. "I didn't 'sustain' it so much as have one serious SOB hit me over the head with a chair so that he could escape from a murder scene." *Only Sean had still been alive then…if I hadn't gotten knocked out, maybe he could have received help in time.*

"Your symptoms can include dizziness..."

Check, he had that.

"Slurred speech..."

Right, he'd been plenty slurred in the ambulance.

"You could black out again."

He hoped to hell not. He had work to do. *I've got to find Henry.* But first, he needed to see Jamie. There were some things he had to tell her before anything else happened.

Like... *I love you.* Scary words. Words he'd never said to another lover, but words he was determined to say to her.

When you woke up in a pool of your own blood...with a dead man just a few feet away... well, a guy's priorities could line up, real fast.

Priority number one for him was telling Jamie exactly how he felt about her.

He reached for his clothes. If necessary, he'd walk out of there with his butt bare and that hospital gown flapping around him, but he'd prefer to be—

"You could have a seizure!" Her voice had sharpened. "This isn't some game, sir! It's your life."

He thought of the battles he'd faced. The wounds that still marked him.

And he thought of Jamie.

She's my life.

The door to his room flew open. Grant was there, his eyes a bit wild, and Mac was right behind him.

Some of the tension eased from Davis's shoulders. Mac had gone to get Jamie. "Is she outside?" Davis asked. "Tell her to come in." *I need to see her. I need to touch Jamie. I have to make sure she's all right.*

But Mac paled.

Grant cleared his throat and stepped into the room. "Doctor, would you give us a minute alone?"

"Fine," the doctor snapped. She pointed toward Davis. "Maybe during that minute, you can talk some sense into this man. The *last* thing he needs to do is leave the hospital now." She bustled out of the room.

Davis pulled on his clothes. He ignored the dizziness and nausea. *Jamie's close. Jamie is—*

"Davis, I'm going to need you to stay calm," Grant said, his words slow and quiet. "You know we'll have your back. We'll find her."

Find...her? Davis turned his head and focused on Mac. "Jamie's outside. She's in the waiting room."

"No." Mac stared at Davis, still pale, his eyes tormented. "I'm sorry."

Davis took a staggering step toward him. "Where's Jamie?" His voice came out rusty, rough. Lost.

Because he felt lost right then. Lost and confused. Angry and afraid. He could feel something clawing at him from the inside, sharp and hard, clawing to get out.

"Where. Is. Jamie?"

Mac shook his head. "I don't know. He... he took her."

A ringing filled Davis's ears. That clawing inside got even worse, and he knew what it was—fear and fury were fighting to get out. To break loose. "No."

"I left her. When I found out that you were hurt at that motel, I raced away. I thought she was safe at her clinic. Sylvia was there. Patients were scheduled and I—" He broke off. "No, I *didn't* think. I just reacted. You're my brother, and you were all I thought about."

"Jamie."

"Sylvia said he took her. That he..." Mac's gaze cut to a grim-looking Grant. "He injected her with something and tossed her into your rental car. They raced away, and the cops—the cops have an APB out now. I gave them Henry's description. They're searching all the roads. They will find her."

But would she still be alive then? Was she even alive now?

"I am so sorry," Mac said. "I'll make this right. I swear."

The fury kept clawing at him. So did the fear. "I love her." He needed to tell Jamie.

"I know," Mac said, his voice roughening even more. "I *will* make this right."

Jamie. Have to find Jamie.

But where would Henry take her?

He walked toward the door. His steps were too slow, and he hated that. His body wasn't quite listening to him, not yet. But it would. He grabbed for the door and wrenched it open. The doctor was still in the hallway, and she spun toward him.

"No!" Her gaze slid over his shoulder, to Grant and Mac. "You two were supposed to talk sense into him. He shouldn't go anywhere."

Henry has Jamie.

"Sorry, doctor," Grant said. "But I don't think anything can keep him here now."

Davis stalked toward the elevator. *Is this why you left me alive, you jerk? Because you knew it would tear out my heart when I discov-*

ered that you'd taken Jamie? You wanted me to suffer, so you left me alive in that motel room?

His brothers followed him into the elevator. Davis jabbed the button for the ground floor.

"Henry called her," Mac said, his voice still too rough. "He said that you and Sean were in the motel room. That you'd been hurt, and—"

"I was bait." Henry had been watching him. Had been watching Sean. *He beat me to the motel room.* "He used me so that she'd be vulnerable." *He knows my family. Knows all of our weaknesses.*

"According to Sullivan," Grant said as the elevator doors opened, "Henry has been missing from the psychiatric facility in Connecticut for at least a month. He's got some actor up there that he hired as his double, a guy that he's been using on and off for years to play him."

While he slips way...and does what? Searches for Jamie?

"If he's been gone a month, then he could have been down here that whole time. Watching her." Waiting for his moment to close in. "He'd need a place to stay for that long." It was so hard to think with the constant throbbing of his head, but he pushed that pain aside. "He'd want to be somewhere close to Jamie." *Close to Jamie's property?*

And he remembered the motorcycle. The night her house had burned, the motorcycle and its rider had been hidden behind the trees near her house.

Were you that close all along? Was it even possible? "Get…get property maps," he said slowly. "Call local Realtors… I want to know the closest homes to Jamie's property. I don't care if they are one-room cabins…if something is out there, I want to know."

Grant immediately pulled out his phone. "You really think he'd just take her right back to that place? I mean, *if* he has a place that close? Shouldn't he run away with her?"

"The goal isn't to run." That was the part that scared him the most. "The goal is for him to never let her go."

Henry wouldn't want to run. He'd just want to be alone with Jamie. And, when he was ready, Henry would want to kill her.

Davis strode forward.

But Mac caught his arm. "I'm sorry. You asked me for one thing…just to keep her safe…"

Mac. He was called the wildest of the bunch for a reason. Emotion and impulse had always ruled him.

"I should have taken her with me," Mac whispered. "I was just so worried about getting to you, I didn't stop to think. I didn't want to lose another member of my family." Pain twisted his face. "But now——"

"I'm not going to lose her," Davis said. "I can't." Fury and fear...they'd battled within him. One had finally pierced to freedom. Fury. Because the fear couldn't win. If it did, he'd be helpless. But the fury, oh, it gave him strength. Power. "I am going to find Jamie. I am going to take her away from Henry, and I will make sure that he *never* hurts anyone else again." Henry was about to see just how dark and deadly the McGuires could be.

You hurt one of us, and we all come down on you in a fury.

A damn fury.

"Now let's find out which houses are close to Jamie's place. I don't care if ten miles is the closest one... I want the listings. And we are going to search every single place. We are going to keep searching until we find her." They *would* find her.

Because if they didn't...

No. "We will find her."

HENRY HADN'T STABBED HER.

He'd hauled Jamie inside the old house. She'd had a fast, fleeting impression of wood painted white, a slanting roof, a place that looked as if time had forgotten it...

Then they were inside. Only the inside wasn't dusty and empty. There was furniture. New furniture that smelled of leather. Lights. A TV. Computers.

He's been living here?

"I know, I know..." Henry said, glancing around. "It's an extreme fixer-upper, but we're really not going to be here long enough for a complete overhaul. So I just brought in the comforts of home. I mean, I needed a few things while I waited for you."

"Waited for me?"

He shoved her down on the couch. Her hands and feet were still bound, and the rough rope had made her wrists start to bleed. Well, they'd bled when she pulled and pulled, desperate to escape her restraints.

He paced in front of her. "I wasn't sure how to approach you at first. Did I want to go to the clinic? Come see you at home?" He sighed. "So at first, I just watched..."

And she remembered the strange awareness she'd felt for the past few weeks. The nervousness. *He was there and I didn't realize it.*

"I was coming to talk to you... I was ready for you again..." His face hardened. He had changed so little in the passing years. She could see flashes of the boy she'd known, but then, the terrifying man he'd become would push through. "And you brought *him* home with you."

Davis. "Did you kill him?" That was what mattered to her. Was Davis alive or was he dead?

"One lover was dead when I left." He smiled. "But don't worry. I planned well. Sean was the one I gutted."

She flinched. Her scars seemed to burn. *Will he be gutting me soon, too?*

"Don't you think he deserved it?" Henry asked, voice almost musing. "I mean, for all that he did to you. He betrayed you, Jamie. Lied to you. Lied about you. All for money."

She shook her head. "No, no, I don't think he deserved it." Who deserved that?

"I know what Davis deserves." Now his face hardened even more. His eyes blazed. "Pain. So much pain. He'll have my life. The life I knew when you were gone. No matter how hard he searches, he won't find you. He'll know that he lost you. That you slipped right through his fingers. You didn't want him. You wanted *me*."

She stared up at him. "You aren't serious." *Davis is alive! He's alive!* And she wasn't going down without a fight. "I don't want you, Henry."

A furrow appeared between his brows.

She held up her bound hands. "Have you lost touch with reality that much? You drugged me. You kidnapped me. I don't want to be with you. I *hate* you."

"No, no, you loved me once—"

"I was seventeen. You were my first—"

"Yes." He smiled. "Your first. Should have been only."

"My first serious boyfriend." She made her voice ice cold. "But I didn't love you. Not even then. I knew the truth. Why do you think I broke up with you?" *You were scaring me. You were too controlling.*

"You loved me then." He seemed utterly confident. "You'll love me again. We'll have so much time together. I'll make you love me."

Goose bumps rose on her arms. He sounded as if he had some very long-term plans happening. "Davis will look for me."

"Yes. Look but never find. It took me all these years to find you. Searching. You vanished, and I *hurt*."

Good. He'd hurt her plenty, too. "You killed my brother. You tried to kill me. What did you expect me to do? Marry you?"

He blinked. "I—I was only punishing you." He looked down at the knife in his hand. "You had to see that you were mine. So I marked you, so that you'd always know."

She nearly vomited right then. "Marked me? I was in the hospital for three days. You attacked me! And my brother—"

"He shouldn't have gotten in the way. If he'd stayed back, he would be alive. It's his fault."

A chill enveloped her. "I loved my brother."

He shrugged.

"I didn't love you."

In a flash, he'd lunged across the room. He put the knife at her throat, and the blade nicked her skin. She could feel a drop of blood sliding down her neck. "Don't say that."

She didn't say anything at all.

"You did love me once. You will love me again."

No.

"It's just us now, Jamie. Always…us." He pressed a kiss to her cheek but didn't move the blade from her throat. "Before you know it, you won't even be able to imagine a life without me in it."

She was afraid to swallow, because she didn't want that knife to slice her.

"He won't find you." His smile held a touch of pity. "So you should give up that hope."

No, she shouldn't. Because Davis wasn't Henry. Davis was a professional investigator, and she knew with utter certainty that he wouldn't give up on her.

She just had to stay alive long enough for Davis to find them.

Just stay alive...

Easier said than done.

"You don't love him," Henry said. "I know you don't. Tell me you don't love him."

The blade dug into her skin. "Does your father know what you're doing?" Jamie asked, trying to distract him.

"My father?" His lips twisted. "He's a fool. Too tied up with his business and his image to know anything. He wanted me to stay away from you. I'd hire PIs to find you, and then he'd fire them. Always in my business. Always watching me. But I found a way around him..."

He crouched down in front of her.

She pushed back on the couch, trying to put distance between them.

"Want to know my secret?"

She really didn't want to know anything about him.

"I've got a twin." He put his index finger to his lips and gave a low, "Shhh…"

He didn't have a twin. He—

"I pay him to be me. To pretend. No one gets close. No one knows. So I was able to slip away. To find you." The knife had moved away, and she could actually breathe again. "No one even knows that I'm here. They'll never be able to pin Sean's murder on me."

So he was sane enough to have planned all of this. Sane enough to have an alibi in place…

But enough of a monster that he'd still committed so many terrible acts.

"I'm so glad you were looking for me, too," he whispered.

"I wasn't looking for you." Jamie wished she could have taken those words back. She was playing this scene wrong. If she wanted to live, she should be telling him what he wanted to hear.

But I can't. I—

"You sent me letters. Sent my father letters. Saying you'd never forget." His smile was tender now. "I tracked down those notes and the flowers."

Flowers?

"You kept them until they died…because

they were *our* flowers. I gave you roses on all of our dates. I remembered. So did you."

She hadn't remembered. She'd tried so hard to forget.

"The florist…she described you. I knew you were trying to send me a message, so I made it my mission to find you."

I didn't. I didn't!

"And now you're here," he said. His fingers stroked her cheek. "We can be together. Always."

"So we're going in hard and fast?" Grant asked as he checked his weapon.

"Hell, yes," Davis snapped. The dizziness had passed. Only his fury remained. They were about fifty yards away from the white house—the house with the peeling paint. The house that was adjacent to Jamie's property. The place had been on the market for years.

But the home had sold a few weeks ago. A cash purchase. And Davis knew with utter certainty who'd moved into that home.

"We can wait for the cops," Mac said, his voice quiet. They were all being quiet because the last thing they wanted to do was tip off the guy inside. "They'll be here in ten minutes."

"What if she doesn't have ten minutes?"

He didn't know what was happening in that building. Jamie could need him. Henry could be hurting her. She could—

He heard a scream. High-pitched, desperate. Coming from inside that house. Davis didn't hesitate. He shot up from the cover of the trees and ran as fast as he could.

Hold on, Jamie! Hold on, sweetheart. I'm coming for you.

THE BLADE STABBED into Jamie's shoulder, and she screamed because she hadn't expected the attack. One minute, Henry had been smiling at her. Telling her about the "always" that they would have together. And the next...

He'd stabbed her.

"You distracted me," Henry growled at her now. "Just realized...you never said... you never said you didn't love him, Jamie."

He pulled the blade out. The pain was white-hot, burning. Exactly as she remembered. She'd never forgotten the feel of a knife slicing into her.

"Say you don't love him, Jamie." He was crouched right above her. That knife dripping with her blood. The blade so very sharp. *"Say it!"*

"Untie my hands."

He blinked.

"Untie my hands. Cut the rope away from my feet."

He lifted the knife, seemingly ready to stab her again.

"Do you love me?" Jamie asked him, rushing out those words.

The knife froze. "Yes, yes, of course I do."

He was even more unstable now than he'd been before.

"Don't you want me to hold you? To hug you? It's been so long since we've been together…" If she could get him to slice away the ropes, then she'd have a fighting chance. "I'm not going to run." *Yes, yes I am. As fast as I can.* "Cut the ropes."

He looked at the knife. Then at her ropes. And he actually started to slice at the ropes around her feet. *Yes!*

The ropes gave way, and feeling rushed back to her feet. It was painful, like pins were being pushed into her soles.

Footsteps were pounding. Racing outside.

"Jamie!" Her name was a roar of anger and fear.

Shock rippled across Henry's face, and then he was lunging upright. He spun toward the front door just as it was kicked open. Davis stood there, filling the doorway, his chest heaving. Mac and Grant were right behind him.

"No!" Henry yelled. He grabbed Jamie. Put the knife to her throat. "You don't get to have her! Stay back! Stay away or I will slice her throat open!'

Davis froze. His gaze jerked to Jamie's. He looked so pale. She could see blood on his shirt. The faint lines on his face were deeper, and he seemed so haggard as he gazed at her.

"Jamie," Davis whispered. There was so much emotion in his voice. So much longing.

Henry yanked her back, and they stumbled around the couch. Her hands were still bound, but her feet were free.

Davis had his gun up and aimed—aimed at Henry's head because the rest of the guy's body was behind her. *He's using me as his shield.*

Mac and Grant were armed, too. And they'd slid around a few feet, moving deeper into the house.

She had the feeling that as soon as one of those men felt they had a clear shot, they'd be taking it.

More blood. More death.

"It doesn't have to be this way," Jamie said. She hurt for them all in that moment. Her brother. Herself. Even Henry. Things could have been so different for everyone. "Let me go, Henry. You can get help, you can—"

"They *can't* help me. They can't fix what's wrong. Not with the drugs or the therapy. I don't want to be fixed! I *like* the way I feel..." His hold hardened on her. "I'm all powerful. You're going to see that, Jamie. They're all going to see it."

"Let her go," Davis said.

But Henry called back, "Drop your guns or I will slit her throat right in front of you."

Davis hesitated.

"If you love her," Henry blasted. "Drop the gun! Make them all drop their guns!"

And Davis dropped his gun.

Tears slid down Jamie's cheeks.

"Drop the guns," Davis said to his brothers.

They lowered their weapons.

"Kick them all toward me," Henry immediately ordered.

They did.

"Now let her go," Davis said. "You've got what you want—"

"Not yet, I don't." In a lightning fast move, Henry dropped the knife and scooped up one of the weapons. Davis's gun. He aimed that gun at Davis. "Jamie, tell him that you don't love him."

She stared into Davis's eyes.

"Tell him."

He was going to kill Davis. She knew it with utter certainty. It didn't matter what she said.

So I'll just tell him the truth.

"Davis…"

He shook his head. "No, sweetheart…" Davis sounded tormented.

"I love you." So simple. So true.

"What? *No!*" And Henry whirled her toward him. That was what she'd wanted. For him to take his aim off Davis. To focus on her. "You can't! You love me!"

Jamie threw her body at him. They collided in a tangle of limbs, and the gun exploded.

Chapter Thirteen

When the gun fired, Davis felt his heart stop. *Jamie, please, no!* He flew across the room. Henry had risen, and the bastard was aiming his gun again. Preparing to fire at Jamie as she lay on the floor. She was bleeding. He could see the blood soaking her shirt, and fury drove him to the edge. He caught Henry's hand. Snapped the guy's wrist. The gun fell to the floor, and Davis punched him.

Again.

Again.

He heard bones crunch when he broke Henry's nose.

Henry was trying to fight back. Punching and clawing, but Davis wasn't going to be stopped. This was the man who'd hurt Jamie. The man who'd made her life a hell.

The man who tried to take her from me. He wasn't going to stop. He'd—

Mac pulled him back. Henry sagged to his

knees on the floor, not fighting any longer. Hardly seeming to move any longer.

"She's okay," Mac told him.

Davis just stared at Henry. *Destroy.*

Mac shook him hard. "She's okay! The bullet didn't hit her. I think—he must have stabbed her. That's why she screamed before. Look. *Look.*" He jerked Davis's head to the right. Grant had pulled Jamie to the side. As Davis watched, his older brother kept applying pressure to a wound on Jamie's shoulder. Jamie stared back at Davis, dazed. "She's alive, man," Mac told him. "You found her. She's safe."

He shoved Mac back and ran to Jamie. Her hands were still tied, and he yanked at the ropes to free her. Then her hands slipped around him. She kissed him. He kissed her. He felt some of the terrible fear and fury slide back enough so that he could think.

Jamie. My Jamie is with me.

"I knew you'd find me," she told him, voice husky. "He said you wouldn't, but I knew…"

He pulled back, just enough to stare into her eyes.

"I trust you," she said.

"And I love you," Davis told her. He kissed her again. Held her tight. So tight. He never wanted to be that afraid again. He never wanted to be apart from her.

He needed Jamie. Her smiles. Her warmth. Her wit.

Her.

"You can't love him!"

Davis stiffened at Henry's sharp cry.

"Jamie, you can't. I don't know why you lie."

Davis pulled Jamie close. He helped her rise to her feet, and they turned to face Henry. Mac had a gun aimed at him, but Henry wasn't looking at the weapon.

His gaze was focused totally on Jamie.

Blood dripped from his broken nose, but he ignored that, too. He ignored everything but Jamie. He was curled on the floor, his body hunched over, but his eyes locked on Jamie.

"You'll always love me," he told her as he slowly began to uncurl his body and stand. "Just as I'll always love you. No one will keep us apart. I'll see to that." He smiled. "So they give me *therapy* again. It will slow me down for…what? A few months? Maybe a year? Then I'll be out again. I'll find you, wherever you go…whatever you do… I'll find you." He was on his feet. "You'll never be free because you'll always be mine. Mine." His hand had slipped down inside of his shirt, as if he were reaching for something.

He'd been curled on the floor—dammit, the knife! Had the guy reached for the discarded weapon?

Davis tensed and tried to push Jamie behind him. Where had the guy put the knife from earlier? Where—

"Always, mine!" Henry shouted, and he yanked a knife from under his shirt. He lunged at Davis and Jamie.

"No!" The terrified shout came from behind Henry.

But... Henry ignored the shout.

Once again, gunfire blasted.

And Henry couldn't ignore the gunfire... because the bullet had hit him in the chest.

Henry staggered. The knife was still in his tight grip as he looked down at his chest. "J-Jamie?"

Davis had pushed her behind him. He'd been ready to take the hit from that knife but...

But Mac had fired before Henry could hurt anyone else.

Henry's knees sagged, and he fell to the floor.

"No!" It was the same desperate cry that

Davis had heard before the gunfire. A cry coming from the open front door.

An older man rushed into the house. His brown hair was tousled, as if he'd raked his hand through it over and over, his eyes, the same shade of ice-blue as Henry's, were wild with grief and pain. He fell to the floor beside Henry, and he rolled his body over. "Henry, no!"

Sullivan rushed into the house behind the stranger. His gaze flew around the room, and he exhaled in relief when he saw his brothers.

Then he strode toward Davis.

"I need an ambulance!" the older man yelled.

Jamie slipped around Davis. She stared at Henry's prone body. He was still alive but bleeding heavily.

"We came in quietly," Sullivan muttered. "Just in case..." He looked back at Henry, and his face tensed. "His father and I both got into the airport at the same time. We flew in on the guy's jet and got here as fast as we could. Garrison over there—he located this place on the ride here. Seems Henry bought it under one of the company's umbrella accounts."

Grant stalked toward Mac. Mac still had his weapon in his hand. Grant's fingers closed around Mac's shoulder.

"I couldn't let him hurt our brother," Mac said, his voice wooden. "I couldn't."

Cops came spilling into the house then. Earlier, Mac had said they were ten minutes out, and it looked as though that had been true.

Ten minutes...

Too late.

The cops took the weapon from Mac. He put his hands up.

"He had to shoot!" Jamie cried out. "Henry had a knife. He wasn't going to stop. He would have killed me."

She spoke with such certainty. And Davis realized that, deep down, Jamie had always realized that truth. Henry Westport had been fixated on her since she was a teenager. He'd never had any intention of letting Jamie go.

When Davis glanced at the older man—Henry's father—he saw the older man flinch. *You knew he'd kill her, too.* Maybe that was why the guy had gone looking for Sean Nyle. Because he was trying to stop the monster already in motion.

Davis wrapped his arm around Jamie. "She needs medical treatment!"

"I need you," Jamie whispered. The EMTs were rushing toward her, but she turned in his arms. "I didn't think I'd see you again."

"Ma'am…" one of the EMTs began. "Ma'am, that's a lot of blood loss."

Yes, it was. "Go with them, sweetheart." He leaned down. Kissed her. "I'll be with you." Letting her out of his sight anytime soon? *Not* a possibility. Hell, no.

He'd never been that afraid, and he hadn't even realized he'd had so much to lose. Not until Jamie was gone.

She smiled at him. A beautiful sight, one that made his heart ache. The EMT led her through the house. Davis followed right behind her.

"This stays out of the news, do you hear me?" The older man was snapping to the cop even as he kept his gaze on Henry's prone form. EMTs were examining him, but Davis knew there was nothing that could be done. "I don't want a word of this leaking to the media. My son will not be remembered as—"

Something snapped in Davis right then. He grabbed the guy, his hands fisting in his shirt-front. "He kidnapped her!"

Jamie turned to look back at him.

"He drugged her. He stabbed her."

The man's eyes widened.

"Look around, dammit! This isn't some romantic getaway. He had her tied up. He had a knife to her throat when I burst into this room. You want the world to think of him as a saint? Too bad. That's not happening. And you know what else? He's not the only one at fault." Fury bit through each word. "You paid people to lie. You bought his freedom when you *knew* he was dangerous. You could have stopped this...you could have saved her brother's life. You could have saved Sean Nyle." He looked over at Henry. "And maybe you could have even saved *him* if you hadn't been so damn concerned with your image." An image he was about to see wrecked just as he'd wrecked—

"Davis..." Jamie whispered. "Please...you said you'd come with me." She lifted her hand toward him. Her fingers shook. "I just want to be with you."

A shudder shook him as he fought to get his rage under control. Then he nodded. And he took her hand. But he sent one last glare at his prey. "I will be seeing you again." No way did that guy get to escape scot-free for the things he'd done.

His fingers twined with Jamie's. *Jamie.* Safe. Alive. With him.

They climbed into the back of the ambulance. The EMT started cutting away Jamie's shirt.

As she was lowered onto the stretcher inside, Jamie's head turned and her gaze met his. "I don't have to be afraid anymore, do I?"

"No, sweetheart, you don't."

"No more ghosts." Again, that faint smile curved her lips.

"No more ghosts," he agreed. If he had his way, she'd only know joy for the rest of her life.

"I knew you'd come," Jamie said. "I figured...I just had to stay alive long enough for you to arrive."

What if she hadn't? His fingers tightened around hers. "When they told me you were gone..." *My world stopped, Jamie. Everything stopped for me.* He cleared his throat. "Jamie—"

The siren screamed on. He looked through the open doors of the ambulance. Grant had walked outside, and his brother's stare was on him. Mac stood a few feet away, talking with some uniformed cops.

Mac had killed to protect Jamie. When it came to family, you'd do anything necessary.

Jamie is family. She's everything to me.

The doors slammed shut.

"Jamie..." Davis cleared his throat. This wasn't the right time, he knew that. But today he'd learned that waiting would do no good. There was no perfect moment in life. Never a perfect time. There was just the here and now, and to be happy, you had to seize that moment—*right then*. "Jamie, I meant what I said before. I love you."

He wanted her to know that. To understand—always.

"I love you, too," she whispered back.

The ambulance rushed forward, and they left her past behind.

HENRY WESTPORT WAS DEAD. She'd never look into the shadows and wonder if he was lurking there. Never nervously peer over her shoulder to see if he was following her. He was gone.

"I'm sorry," Mac said.

Jamie glanced over at him. They were at McGuire Securities headquarters—her, Davis, Mac, Brodie, Jennifer, Grant and Grant's wife, Scarlett. The whole group had assembled. Two days had passed since her abduction. Two days of talking to cops, of answering hundreds of questions and of putting her past to rest. Finally.

"Sorry?" Jamie repeated. "You saved us! You—"

"It's my fault you were taken." Mac stared down at his fisted hands. "I didn't think, I just reacted when I heard about Davis. My job was to protect you, and I failed."

She walked to him. Davis stood a few feet away, watching silently.

Jamie hugged Mac. "You didn't fail at anything. I… I didn't tell you the truth." Her confession time. She'd already told this part to the cops, but not to Mac. She pulled back and stared into his eyes. "When Henry called me, he offered an exchange. He said he'd leave Davis and Sean—just as they were." *One alive, one dead.* "If I came to him. He told me where to meet him, and he told me that I had to come right then."

Mac's eyes widened.

"I didn't tell you that part. I just told you to go after Davis because he was what mattered to me."

"Dammit, Jamie…" Davis swore.

Right. He hadn't heard this part yet, either.

"Henry would have kept coming after me," Jamie said. "And you rushing to keep your brother alive—that wouldn't have changed things. I *wanted* you to go after Davis. Because I needed him to be safe." Her gaze slid to Davis. "I rather like the world more, when he's in it."

The door opened then. Jamie turned and

found Sullivan standing in the doorway. Only…he wasn't alone.

Garrison Westport stood just behind him.

"What the hell?" Davis snarled. He lunged forward. "Get that guy out of here!"

Jamie grabbed his arm, pulling him back. Sure, she might feel the exact same way about Garrison Westport but—

"He has something to say that I think you all need to hear," Sullivan said. A muscle jerked near his jaw. "After that, we can all kick him out."

Garrison—looking tired and pale and much older than he'd looked just days before—crept into the office.

His gaze flew all around the room, seeming to dart everywhere…except to Jamie. Or Mac.

"He did it," Sullivan announced.

Davis shot forward—Jamie tightened her hold on him, trying to keep him from attacking the guy.

"He's the one," Sullivan said, "who pulled strings at the US Marshal's office…he got Jamie her new life. Well, it was him and her father. They worked together back then."

Her father?

Garrison's head bowed. "Not that it did much good."

Jamie shook her head. "What?"

"When I was in Connecticut, I paid a little visit to your father. I was already a bit confused about the US Marshal's involvement—I mean, your case isn't the type that would normally get you protection from their office."

He saw my father?

"Your dad admitted that he'd been the one to contact the US Marshal's office, only he had help." Sullivan's gaze slanted toward Garrison. "In order for you to get your new life, a whole lot of money changed hands."

Garrison had always been good at tossing his money around. *And he used that money on me?* She'd used his blood money and hadn't even known it.

Garrison wasn't looking at her, and Jamie couldn't take her eyes off him.

"When he killed your brother..." Garrison's gaze was directed toward the floor as he began to slowly speak. His fancy suit was wrinkled. "I knew...I knew his obsession with you wasn't going to stop. I knew he was a threat. But he was my son, and a father is supposed to watch out for his son..."

"He hurt me," Jamie whispered. "You made everyone doubt my story. Made my own parents turn from me...."

"I'm sorry," Garrison rasped. "I didn't know what else to do—Henry was *my* family and I—" He broke off, seemingly unable to say more.

Maybe there was no more to say. The guy had been given a choice—Jamie or Henry. He'd chosen his flesh and blood over her life.

"When your father came to me, demanding protection for you, I called in favors. I paid more money than, well…I paid as much as necessary. I got you a new life. I thought you would be safe. I thought you'd be happy."

"Look at me," Jamie demanded.

Garrison's gaze rose.

"When did you realize he was after me again? When did you realize he'd found me?"

Garrison's gaze cut to Sullivan.

"Me," Jamie demanded, anger sharpening her voice. "I'm here. The woman your son tried to destroy. Do me the courtesy of looking me in the eyes."

Garrison nodded. "Your mother—"

Her mother? First, her father and now, her mother? She'd thought they'd written her off years before.

"She began writing to me. She wanted to know where you were. Hated living in the past and needed you, and she blamed me for everything. Henry found one of her notes, but he thought it was from you. I saw the obsession kick to life again, like a match striking. And then I started checking all of the accounts. Money was missing. He'd hired people to find you over the years, but, luckily, I'd learned about most of them. I fired them, and no one seemed to ever get close to you. The US Marshals had been so good at their jobs."

And I kept running. Never staying in one place too long. Until I came here.

"About a month ago, his behavior became more...erratic. That's when I contacted Sean Nyle. I needed to make sure you were safe. And you seemed to be. Henry—at that same time, he told me that he was going to check himself in for more counseling. He told me that he realized he was sick again." He stepped toward her. "I believed him! I thought he was better—he was recognizing that he was getting out of control. I never imagined that he was just tricking me..."

"He fooled you for a long time."

His shoulders stiffened. "Yes, he did. He hired an actor—"

"One he'd been using for years," Sullivan threw in.

Garrison paled even more. "He'd been

hunting for you, all that time, and using that man to cover for him when he needed to disappear."

Davis growled. "He won't ever hunt her again."

"No." Garrison's voice had gone hoarse. "He won't." His stare held Jamie's. "I'm sorry."

She could only gaze blankly back at him.

"I want to make this up to you," Garrison said quickly. "I will pay for your house to be rebuilt, I can pay to expand your clinic, I can pay—"

"You can't pay," Jamie gritted out, "to make pain disappear. I don't want your money. I don't want anything from you. Just get out of my life." Because he was a reminder of the past that she never wanted to see again.

She wanted to think about her future. About hope.

Not hell.

His lips trembled, and the guy seemed legitimately confused. As if he couldn't understand why she didn't just let him throw money at her.

"Information," he said suddenly, snapping his fingers. "That's what I can give you." His gaze—slightly feverish now, with desperation—swept over them all. When he looked at Mac, he paled even more, and a long shudder shook his body. "You don't even know... but I do! I can help you!" He nodded quickly.

But Davis marched toward him. "We don't want any help from you." He pointed to the door. "Sullivan, he's done here. Take him out."

Sullivan opened the door.

"But—*your parents*!"

Everyone seemed to freeze then.

"I know...all about your mother."

Jamie's gaze snapped up toward Davis. His face had locked down, but his eyes blazed with fury.

"The same US Marshal I used...I, um, I may have paid an investigator to break into his files. It was just when I needed to make sure Jamie was still safe!" His words tumbled out at a frantic rate. "Only...when I was accessing those files, I learned more."

Now Grant strode toward him. "You mean when you were breaking into secure government files? Committing an *illegal* act?" He made a sound of disgust. "I think we're done. My family doesn't need you jerking us around any longer—"

Sullivan clapped a hand on his shoulder. "You're done now, Westport."

"She was in the Witness Protection Program! Her name came up… I was cross-refer-encing when I found out from Sean Nyle that Jamie had moved to Austin. Your *mother*…"

Now he was shaking as he continued, "She came here when she was twenty. She was originally Ada Gregory—she came here—"

Sullivan spun him around. "This better not be some line."

"It's not! I have the files. I can give them to you." Garrison smiled weakly. "That makes up for it, doesn't it? For the things I did?"

Jamie's stomach clenched.

But Davis pulled her close. Hugged her tight. "Not even close. *Get him out of here.*"

And Sullivan pushed Garrison out of the door. The others glanced at Jamie, at Davis, and then they, too, slipped away.

The door closed behind them all. Davis didn't let Jamie go. He held her even more tightly. "There is nothing in this world," Davis said softly, "worth more to me than you are. Nothing. Do you understand?"

His eyes were holding hers, that green stare so deep and true.

Jamie nodded.

"I want to spend my life with you. I want to be with you, always. When you're ready for more, for the next step, you tell me. For now, I'll just be…here. Loving you."

The next step. Marriage? Family?

Jamie wet her lips. "I'll be here, always," she told him, her heart racing, "Loving you." Whatever came their way—any threats, any secrets, any sins from the past—they'd face them. She knew that now. They'd face everything together.

Together, they were stronger. Together, they were happier.

Together, they could defeat any darkness that came their way.

Epilogue

Everyone loved a good wedding. Well, nearly everyone.

Jamie was so nervous that her stomach ached. Her hands were shaking, and she'd pretty much shredded the bouquet.

She wasn't having some big, elaborate affair. That wasn't what she'd wanted. She'd just wanted to marry Davis, to be with him.

His family was there—his brothers, his sister, his sisters-in-law. His family—now hers.

And...her parents were there. Because Sullivan had told Jamie more about her mother's pain. About her father's grief. Too many years had passed. They'd all changed. Jamie had decided that maybe...maybe they should all have a second chance. Would that chance work? Only time would tell.

"You may kiss the bride."

He turned toward her, and Jamie was just so relieved. They'd made it through the ceremony. She'd done it—and Davis was leaning forward. He was going to kiss her. He was going to—

He stopped and stared into her eyes. "I love you."

She smiled at him. "I love you, too."

He kissed her. Probably not the light peck that the Justice of the Peace had been expecting. Hard and deep and sensual.

And when he pulled back, Davis whispered, "So...who do you want to hit with your bouquet? I know how much you like slamming it around in a crowd."

His words were so unexpected that Jamie laughed. And when she laughed, the last bit of her fear and pain slipped away. This was a day of new beginnings. A day of joy.

This was her day. She lifted her bouquet. No single ladies were there, but there were a few single men. She sized up her prey.

And she threw the bouquet right at Mac.

* * * * *